"Magical, strange and utterly lovely, while still deeply rooted in the sweat, dirt, and grief of one hot Texas summer. An extraordinary read—I had to tear myself away from it."
—Katherine Catmull, author of *Summer and Bird*

"More than a modern fairytale retelling, in *Nightingale's Nest*, Loftin constructs a story that tugs and tears at the reader's heart while expertly weaving what remains into a nest as lovely and magical as Gayle's birdsong."
—Bethany Hegedus, author of *Truth with a Capital T* and *Between Us Baxters*

"Nikki Loftin's *Nightingale's Nest* tugs at the mind and at the heart. Riveting from the beginning, it's filled with characters that step out of the book and mysteries that will keep you turning the pages. All the while, remaining a poignant story about loss, love, loyalty and the importance of standing up for what's right. This is a book you'll long remember."
—Lynda Mullaly Hunt, author of *One for the Murphys*

"*Nightingale's Nest* is a lovely, nuanced story as hopeful as it is heart-breaking. . . : Loftin's eye for strange beauty in unexpected places often takes the reader's breath away. It is a story that lingers, bittersweet but ultimately joyous, told by a boy wiser than his years about a girl who is more than she seems."
—Claire Legrand, author of *The Cavendish Home for Boys and Girls*

"*Nightingale's Nest* is a beautiful and lyrical blend of magical realism and timelessness, about a boy desperately trying to do what's right and an extraordinary girl who changes his life forever. Loftin's new novel will haunt your soul—and lift your heart."
—Kimberley Griffiths Little, author of *The Healing Spell* and *When the Butterflies Came*

"*Nightingale's Nest* is a haunting, beautifully told story about the healing power of love, music, friendship, and forgiveness—with just a touch of magic. Nikki Loftin is a remarkable storyteller!"
—Bobbie Pyron, author of *The Dogs of Winter* and *A Dog's Way Home*

"The kind of book I wanted to read slowly. Bittersweet and lovely. *Nightingale's Nest* sings a song of heartbreak and hope."
—Shelley Moore Thomas, author of *The Seven Tales of Trinket*

"Gorgeous and haunting, *Nightingale's Nest* alights in our minds like a deeply-felt dream and does not leave. Loftin's beautifully-rendered contemporary fairy tale looks at the cages we trap ourselves in and shows us how we can finally find our way out. The book reminds us—gently, lovingly—that we cannot always keep the things that are dearest to us, but the joy we got from them can always endure. This is a work of tremendous heart."
—Anne Ursu, author of *Breadcrumbs*

"Sweet, hopeful, and completely lovely, *Nightingale's Nest* perfectly captures the challenges of growing up and dealing with loss. Get ready to have your heart touched."
—Shannon Messenger, author of *Keeper of the Lost Cities*

Nightingale's Nest

Nikki Loftin

razor
bill

An Imprint of Penguin Group (USA) LLC

A division of Penguin Young Readers Group
Published by the Penguin Group
Penguin Group (USA) LLC
345 Hudson Street
New York, New York 10014

USA / Canada / UK / Ireland / Australia / New Zealand / India / South Africa / China
Penguin.com
A Penguin Random House Company

Library of Congress Cataloging-in-Publication Data

Loftin, Nikki.
Nightingale's nest / Nikki Loftin.
pages cm
Summary: In this twist on "The Nightingale," Little John, despite his own poverty and grief,
reaches out to Gayle, an unhappy foster child living next-door who sings beautifully and hides a
great secret.
ISBN: 978-1-59514-623-6 (paperback)
[1. Singing--Fiction. 2. Foster home care--Fiction. 3. Family problems--Fiction. 4. Birds--
Fiction. 5. Magic--Fiction.] I. Title.
PZ7.L8269Nig 2014
[Fic]--dc23
2013047556

Printed in the United States of America

3 5 7 9 10 8 6 4 2

For Lari

Chapter 1

When I first heard Gayle, I couldn't tell if she was a bird or a girl. All I knew for sure was that the music she made wasn't like anything I'd heard before. It was magic.

Even a kid like me could recognize that.

I'd just come from clearing brush on the Emperor's property. He wasn't really an emperor, of course. His name was Mr. Azariah King, but he'd owned a chain of those almost-everything-for-a-dollar stores in our part of Texas for years, called Emperor's Emporiums, so everybody called him the Emperor.

Except for my dad. He hated the man. But not enough to turn down a steady ten-week job for the summer, even if it was almost a hundred degrees most days. Money was money, and our landlord wasn't going to wait until a better job came along, Mom told us. Dad said he wasn't as worried about rent as he was about getting our cable TV hooked up again; he hadn't been able to catch a single baseball game since the end of May.

So Dad, the Big John of Big John's Tree and Brush Removal, had taken the job to work on the Emperor's failing pecan trees, all 104 acres of them. As for me, I was only twelve, but I'd grown seven inches in nine months. Dad said I was old enough and strong enough to learn how to work with trees during summer vacation. And if I messed up, cut too deep into one of the Emperor's pecans and killed it? He said that would serve the money-grubber right.

I didn't care if I killed a tree, either. I thought the world would be a better place if every tree in it was cut down.

The first thing I noticed that day was the birds. They had flown away, like they usually did, at the sound of Dad's chain saw. But I saw that they had all flown in the same direction, and kept going over the Emperor's tall wooden fence to the neighboring property. That property belonged to Mrs. Cutlin, a widowed lady with one jerk of a son about my age, although they always had some other kids hanging around—she fostered orphans. Not because she was the kind of person who cared about kids, or at least I didn't think so. Dad and I had heard her yelling at her son for the past few weeks. When I'd asked Dad about it, he'd said, "Fostering a kid's worth six hundred dollars a month. Whole town knows she needs the money."

Anyway, there was a tree there, a tall sycamore that grew close to the Emperor's fence line, close enough that some of the branches reached over. I was hauling cut limbs to a place that looked about right for a burn pile, and that's when I saw where the birds had gone.

They were perched in the sycamore, hundreds of them. It looked like someone had taken a paintbrush to the thing, what with all the reds and blues—cardinals and scrub jays—in between the wide leaves. Dozens of sparrows sat along the lower branches, mixed in with black-capped chickadees, finches, wrens, and flycatchers. I even counted four painted buntings, with their rainbow coats, before I realized what was wrong.

None of the birds were singing. They weren't making a single sound.

But something was. Or someone.

I'd never heard a song like it before. I couldn't imagine anyone in the world had.

The notes were high and liquid, a honey-soft river of sound that seeped right through me. I stopped when I heard the first notes and just stood there, dropping cedar cuttings at my feet.

The song sailed over the fence, like it was meant for me alone. No words to it. It was pure melody. I felt almost like my feet were lifting away from the ground, that the only thing holding me to earth was my own belief in gravity.

The song went on, and I peered through my watering eyes at the branches. There was something there. Something bigger than a bird. A collection of stacked twigs and branches, bits of twine, and what seemed to be wire wrapped around it all, holding it together. A nest, it looked like. And the sound was coming from inside.

I took a step toward it, and my foot hit a twig.

The birds heard me first, and they all took flight, enormous confetti swirling into the sky.

Then the music stopped, and I felt my heart constrict, like I'd lost something precious.

I took another step, and another, until I could see through the leaves. That's when I realized the singer was a person. A little girl. She was plain, with brown hair the same color as mine. But hers was ratted around her face like she'd never seen a brush, and she had dirt smeared across her cheeks and nose. *Too thin*, I thought, as she climbed over the edge of the bundled mess of sticks and out onto a branch to see me better. She was awfully close to the slender branches that I knew wouldn't hold the weight of a kid, even a skinny little girl.

I had to get her to come down before she hurt herself. But she looked as frightened of me as the birds had been. As if she might fly away like they had, if I spoke too suddenly.

First, I'd have to get her to trust me.

"Who are you?" I asked in my softest voice. "Was that you singing?" As she inched closer, I realized she must be about eight years old.

The same age my sister, Raelynn, had been.

My heart constricted a bit more. "That was you, right?"

She nodded, her head bobbling like a heavy sunflower on a too-narrow stalk, and edged out a bit more on the branch. Her feet were bare, and dirty. Her toes were as thin as the rest of her, and kind of long—she used them to clutch the branch she was on just like a baby bird would.

"It was beautiful," I said, almost whispered. "The most beautiful thing I ever heard."

She blushed a little.

"What's your name?"

She didn't answer. She looked confused, like she wasn't certain what I'd asked.

Maybe she didn't speak English, I thought. Or maybe she was touched, like my grandma used to say when she meant *crazy*. I tried again: "You got a name?"

"Gayle," she said, clearing her throat to repeat the word. Her speaking voice was unsteady, like she wasn't used to talking. "I'm Gayle."

I recognized the roughness of too many tears cried in the sound of her words. It was the same way my own voice had been for a long time.

Something had happened to her, something bad.

I spoke a little louder and tried to smile. "I'm Little John." I lifted my arms, flexed the muscles, and made a constipated/ mad face like one of the Wrestling Federation guys on TV. I knew it made me look ridiculous, lips pulled back from my teeth, my eyes crossed. But I wanted her to laugh at me. "Little, on account of I'm so small and puny."

Laughter spilled down for a split second. "You're not little."

"Sure I am," I said. "It just looks like I'm big from up there. It's a—what do you call it?—an optical illusion. Why don't you come and see for yourself? Climb on down. Careful, though. That rotten tree isn't sturdy enough for an *enormous* girl like you."

The laughter pealed out again, and I saw her reach out to the tree trunk and hug it, of all things. "It's okay," she whispered to the trunk. "You're not rotten." Like it was her friend, and I'd hurt its feelings. Her feet looked unsteady on the high branch, and the leaves all around her were shaking.

I had to get her down. "Stop fooling around," I tried again, wiping away the sweat that was running into my eyes. "It's not safe up there. You're too high." I had an idea. "I'll get you a piece of candy if you come down. Just do it now, all right?"

She had to come down. If she waited any longer, I was going to have a heart attack.

"Okay," she said. But then she didn't move. She just started humming under her breath, the same tune she'd been singing, but softer this time. It still brought tears to my eyes.

At least I thought that's what was happening. It must have been, because as I watched her, and listened to the music, the singing that got louder and louder, clearer and higher and purer, she got . . . fuzzy around the edges. *Her outline was against the sun,* I thought. That's why she seemed to blur. It was awful hot; maybe it was just the flickering mirage of heat lines.

I wiped my eyes again and squinted up at her. The more she sang, the more she seemed to shimmer against the sky, her edges feathering into the background blue.

Her voice was loud now, so loud I couldn't have stopped the sound even by plugging my ears. Through the melody, though, I heard something squeal and slam behind me, on the other side of the fence. A door.

Someone else was listening.

I turned and saw the Emperor, a hundred yards back, standing outside his back door, a deep purple velvety robe flapping around his bony legs. He was staring at the tree, mouth wide open, watching the girl. The sunlight glinted on his wrinkled, wet cheeks. I wondered, for a moment, at the sight of a grown man crying. But her voice . . . it was the kind that could bring anyone to tears, I figured.

Cra-ack! I knew the sound of a branch cracking. I whirled back around.

That's when I realized the girl had to be touched. She hadn't started to come down at all—she'd started to climb out on the branch, toward me. She was perching, hopping like a wren, further and further out on one of the limbs that wouldn't hold her.

I knew what was going to happen next. She was going to go out too far on the branch, and it would snap under her. She would fall, screaming, in a shower of small branches, leaves, and bark.

It was the nightmare I had every night.

I wouldn't be there to catch her. I never made it to the base of the tree in time, my legs too small, too short, my hands reaching out at the ends of arms too weak to hold her anyway.

And I would have to watch her snap like a bough herself, on the ground, the blood as red as a cardinal's wing.

It was the nightmare I'd lived once before.

And the reason I had devoted my life to cutting down every tree in the world.

Every last murderous tree.

The girl screamed as she fell, and I raced to catch her, knowing I would be too late.

Chapter 2

There was no reason I should have caught her. The branches of the sycamore didn't reach that far over the fence, not far enough that she could have fallen down on the Emperor's side.

She must have jumped, that was it. However it had happened, she landed in my arms, a good twelve feet away from the branch from which she'd fallen.

I held her, trying to stop shaking. Trying to blink the grit and bark out of my eyes so they would stop watering. I felt my pounding heart leap through my chest, where I had her cradled like a baby.

I had caught her. Somehow, I had saved her.

She put a small hand on my heart, right over the beating wall. Her dark brown eyes sparkled up at me, like she'd never been in any danger, like she hadn't been scared one bit. "Sounds like you swallowed a drum," she said. "Right here."

I tried to speak but couldn't. I was still gasping for breath. My hands tightened around her, and I shuddered.

"You," I managed. "You little idiot."

I shook her then, shook her until I could hear her eyeballs rattle in their sockets, until she cried out. "You could have died, you know that? Died!"

"I-I-I'm s-s-sorry," she squeaked at last. "I knew you'd catch me. Didn't you know you could catch me, Tree?"

I stopped shaking her. "What did you call me?"

"Tree," she said, softer. "Just . . . you remind me of a tree."

I dropped her like a hot coal. She grunted when she hit the ground. It didn't seem fair that even her grunt was musical, the low notes of a flute. "Don't call me that. Don't ever."

"Why not?" She stood up, dusting herself off. She wore tattered denim shorts, jeans that had been cut off and belted around the waist with an old blue shoelace to hold them up, and a T-shirt that might have been purple fifty washes ago. "You got eyes the same color as pecans. And you're tan as bark. I love trees."

"Well, I hate them," I said. "I'd rather be called—" I stopped, thinking of all the names my dad used when I didn't move fast enough. I'd been called a lot of things, since I'd started helping him out with the business. But this name stung worse than all of those put together. "Just call me Little John."

"Okay," she rasped out, her voice still rough. Her arms

moved slower as she picked twigs out of her hair. They were the smallest arms I'd ever seen on a girl her age. Thin, and covered with fingerprint-sized bruises. Had I left those? *No,* I thought. Bruises like those took time to purple up.

Maybe she had a mom or dad with hard hands. Maybe there was a reason she had climbed that tree, built that big pile of sticks to hide in.

"Where's your parents, Gayle?" I asked, before I thought better of it.

Her hands stilled. "They flew away," she said softly. Then she leaned up against me, wrapping her arms around my legs like she had with that stupid sycamore.

"Flew away?" I repeated, before I realized. She meant they had died. She was an orphan. "Are the Cutlins fostering you, then?" I asked.

She shivered.

Suddenly, I knew who had left those marks on her arms. Jebediah Cutlin, the kid who had beat on me every year until this one, when I grew tall enough to make him think twice about it.

"Is it just you?" I asked. Maybe she had someone else there, another little girl. A sister, or a brother. Someone to protect her from Jeb. It sure wouldn't be his momma, I knew. She let him get away with anything. The last week of school, he'd stolen twenty dollars right out of our homeroom teacher's purse, and got caught. Our classroom shared a wall with the principal's office, so we'd all heard his mom yelling, blaming our teacher for leaving money out where it was tempting to "rambunctious boys." I'm not sure Jeb even ended up going to detention.

I hated the thought of Gayle alone with the Cutlins, especially Jeb. But sometimes they fostered more than one kid at a time . . .

Gayle shook her head. "Just me," she said, her eyes darting over to the fence.

As if her glance had caused it, a voice called out from the Cutlins' house. "Girl, where you at?" It was Mrs. Cutlin's voice, sharp as a whip crack. Gayle flinched like she had been slapped. "Girl?"

"You better get back home," I whispered, trying to pry the girl off my leg. My fingers got tangled in her hair, and I picked out the twig that had caught my hand. Her hair was soft, softer than any hair I'd ever felt. Familiar, though. I rubbed my fingers through a small lock of it again, wondering where I remembered that texture from.

"Girlie? Get your tail back here!" Mrs. Cutlin's voice was two whip cracks worth of mad now, and Gayle let go of my leg. I could hear a radio blaring out some rock music from inside the house. Mrs. Cutlin had to be standing outside on her porch, but she couldn't see us through the wooden fence. For a second, I thought about grabbing Gayle's hand and running away with her.

Gayle chewed her lower lip as she stared at the fence, then

at me. Maybe she was having the same thought. I shook my head at her.

"You gotta go. I'll give you a boost," I said. "One two three?"

"One two three," she agreed. She stepped one bare foot into my cradled hands, and I lifted her.

"One . . . two . . . !" She had sailed halfway up the fence before I got the last word out.

Either I had gotten a lot stronger in the last few weeks of doing tree work, or she was lighter than any kid should be. "All right, bird bones," I joked. "Stay out of trees from now on. Promise?"

Gayle shook her head, perched on the top of the fence like a chickadee. "I can't. My mom and dad will try to find me. I'm supposed to stay in the nest until they do."

"That nest?" I pointed to the messy pile of twigs and wire.

"Well, it's all I've got. For now." She shrugged and dropped down, disappearing on the other side. I heard her voice as she ran. "Gotta go. But I'll come back and sing for you, Tree—I mean, Little John."

She hummed some tune as she ran, until Mrs. Cutlin's voice cut it short. "Didn't I tell you to stop making that racket?"

A door slammed behind me, and I turned, remembering the Emperor. Had he been outside listening, watching, the whole time? If he had been, he was gone now. I wondered, for a second, how much he could have overheard from where he'd stood.

My dad's chain saw roared again, from the orchard at the side of the house. "Burn pile," I muttered, gathering up the branches I'd dropped. I needed to get my head together; the later it got, the hotter it was going to be for burning brush. But I couldn't stop wondering why that little girl had called me Tree. Couldn't stop thinking about how close she'd come to dying.

And as I picked up the rough, scratching sticks and settled them into a pyramid for a bonfire, I couldn't stop trying to remember where I'd felt anything as soft as her hair.

Chapter 3

I was still thinking about Gayle at breakfast the next morning. Where had she come from? How had her parents died? And how had she jumped that far, so that I could catch her?

"Little John?" I jerked my head up at the sharpness in my mother's voice. "Have you heard a single word I said?"

"No, ma'am," I admitted, glad my dad had gone outside to load up the truck for the day's work. He'd have smacked me for sure, if not for ignoring her, then for being overly honest about it. Mom? She just shook her head. It made the bangs on her forehead fly into her eyes, and she brushed them away with her fork.

I apologized. "What did you say?"

"I said, 'Would you pick up the dead bird outside the garage?' I need you to get rid of it before the cat drags it inside and hides it under the sofa like that last one."

"Yes, ma'am," I said, pushing away from my plate, even

though there was still food on it. I couldn't make myself eat it all. The bacon was overcooked again, and Mom had forgotten to put any salt or sugar in the oatmeal. I didn't say anything, though; bad cooking was the least of the problems we'd had since my sister died. At least this morning, Mom had gotten up and made breakfast, instead of staying in bed until dinnertime, crying and calling out for Raelynn every few seconds.

It was progress, and if it meant I had to choke down some bad food, I'd do it. I'd eat glass if it would make Mom more like herself.

Of course, every time she looked at me, she remembered. She had seemed better during the spring, with me gone every day to school. Now that I was home all the time . . . Maybe I just needed to get gone.

"Mom?" I said, reaching for my work gloves by the back door. "Did you hear about Mrs. Cutlin fostering a girl? I think I saw one over there yesterday."

"I believe I did," Mom said after a few seconds. "At the store, Natalie Mahany said something about a new girl. She said Verlie wasn't sure she could keep this one long—something about her climbing trees and making noise at all hours."

Noise? Was she talking about Gayle's singing, or something else?

Mom went on. "That poor Verlie Cutlin. She's a Christian if I ever saw one. Taking in all those poor little children."

"Verlie Cutlin's not that nice," I said, wondering why all the ladies in the town seemed to think Mrs. Cutlin was some sort of saint for taking in kids. I guess she put on a good act in public. As far as I could tell, when she was alone at home, she hated kids—even her own.

"I've been in prayer circle with her for years, Little John Fischer. That woman has worn her knees out praying for all those foster kids."

I still couldn't see it, but Mom sounded kind of ticked again. Time to change the subject. "I was wondering," I said, "if you'd heard what happened to the girl's parents."

"I can ask. Now you go get that bird before it gets hot and starts to stink." She got up to wash dishes.

I stood there for a second longer. Before Raelynn had died, Mom had always said good-bye with a kiss on my nose. Now I was lucky to get a nod.

Of course, it could have been because I'd grown so tall. She probably couldn't reach my nose anymore.

"I'll see you tonight," I said. "Love you, Mom."

Mom didn't answer. Her back was to me, and she was scrubbing at the skillet like it was stained with something worse than bacon grease.

I went out to get rid of the dead bird.

I didn't mind dealing with birds, alive or dead. I'd spent a long time reading about the kinds of birds that lived in our area. When

I was little, I'd wanted to grow up to be a bird scientist. My grandma told me the word was *ornithologist* and said I could be anything I wanted to be. I think she might even have believed it.

Three years ago, before she died, she had bought me four different bird books for my birthday. The Audubon and Peterson guides were my favorites; they were really expensive ones with color pictures and hard covers. She'd written inside the flaps, *"Love you forever.—Grandma."* Reading them made me feel closer to her, and I took good care of them. Since she was the only grandparent I'd ever known—the rest had died a long time before I was born—I knew I wasn't going to be getting any more bird books. Or anything much else, for that matter.

I'd practically memorized some of them. At first, I'd read so I could answer Raelynn's constant questions about what kind of birds she saw in our backyard. But then it had gotten fun, just to know so much about something nobody else around me did. To be able to listen to a bird sing and recognize its call? To know, from the colors and shape of its wings when it was flying, what kind of bird it was? It made me feel smart.

Of course, I knew I wasn't smart—my report cards from school told the whole world that. And when I'd taken my bird books to show-and-tell, my fourth grade teacher, Mrs. Norman, made sure I knew I wasn't ever going to be an ornithologist. "You can't even spell it, can you, boy?" she'd said. "Be realistic. It takes superior intelligence to pursue that sort of occupation."

She'd liked to use big words; I thought she did it to make me feel dumber.

It worked.

Maybe knowing kinds of birds wouldn't matter to almost anyone—it seemed a sure thing no teacher would ever care. But it had mattered to Raelynn. She'd thought I was the smartest big brother in the world.

The bird Mom sent me to pick up was a barn swallow chick that had fallen from the nest near the corner of the garage. It was small, still covered with downy fluff on its belly. It had to have died that morning; there weren't any ants on it, and it was still warm from the nest. I put my work gloves down and picked it up with one hand, feeling the little neck flop against my thumb. I carried it over to the grass, wondering what to do with it. A year before, I'd have known. Raelynn and I had buried every dead bird and lizard I found with a full ceremony, flowers and a eulogy and all. My next-door neighbor, Ernest, and his little sister, Isabelle, had helped.

Maybe . . . maybe. I could hear the sounds of a car racing game being played inside Ernest's house. I hesitated. Ernest had been my best friend since we were three. But he hadn't come over in months. Not after I'd told him I wasn't interested in playing video games.

It wasn't true. The truth was worse, though. Dad had pawned my game system four months before to cover the light bill. I figured it was better for Ernest to think I was acting mean than to know the truth about how broke we were. And, I mean, what kind of dad sells his kid's Christmas present?

Lots of things like that happened now. It was no use complaining. And it was for the best, I supposed. Isabelle followed Ernest everywhere, now that she didn't have Raelynn.

Isabelle had been Raelynn's best friend, more like a long-lost twin. The two of them had done everything together. Raelynn would even sit in time-out when Isabelle got in trouble, right next to her, just to keep her company. They did their hair the same, wore the same kind of clothes, played the same games. Seeing Isabelle these days always made Mom a little worse.

Even worse than having me around all the time.

I heard Isabelle yelling inside her house. "Turn that off and play Barbies with me, Ernest Wade! I'm gonna tell Mom you're not babysitting me right."

I held back a laugh. Isabelle was the little general of the house, with her momma and daddy wrapped tight as rubber bands around her finger. No matter how Ernest complained, his folks believed every made-up thing his little sister said.

If I didn't do something, Ernest would be playing dolls for a week, no video games at all. I knew just how to save him.

I held one hand up to my mouth and made a loud siren sound, just like an ambulance. I knew how to copy them all— fire trucks, police cars, too. Ernest and I had played this game a lot for the girls, finding sick or hurt animals in the neighborhood. Ernest had wanted to grow up to be a real driver, ambulance or at least UPS, since he was four. Once I gave up on being an ornithologist, I'd decided I might as well be a driver, too. It was fun to imagine Ernest and me, driving around Mills County together for our whole lives. We used to pretend a lot. Ambulance was our favorite game.

We let the girls be the doctors, if it was just a lizard with a tail fallen off or something. But sometimes . . . I peeked through the chain-link fence at Isabelle's graveyard: a dozen or so Popsicle-stick crosses colored with markers and faded glitter glue. My dad had always said Isabelle was "a morbid little thing." She was going to love this.

I let the sound die off with a mournful wail. The coroner's siren. That was our signal for a critter that didn't make it.

"A funeral!" Isabelle screeched like she'd just heard the ice cream truck. "Ernest! Little John's got something dead. Let's go!" There were some crashing noises, and a few screamed words— "Where's my Bible? I can't do it right without a Bible!"—and quick footsteps.

My heart sped up. Maybe I would have time to do the funeral with them. I could gather up some daisies . . . apologize to Ernest somehow for acting so mean. I missed him, bad.

Then Dad's truck horn honked three times in a row, fast and loud. No time. I tossed the bird over Ernest's fence, almost up onto his back porch. I felt bad for a second, just leaving it there. I knew Isabelle would be disappointed I'd taken off. And I sort of hoped Ernest would be, too. Did he miss me? Miss hanging out, talking about video games and NASCAR, school and teachers and normal stuff? I wished I knew. I wished we could go back to what we were like before.

But I took a breath, knowing that wasn't going to happen. At least they would be happy for a while, with or without me. They'd find the bird, Isabelle would keep occupied, and Ernest wouldn't have to play Barbies.

I didn't have time for friends anymore, anyway. I had work to do.

"Are you ready to learn how to seal a cut limb?" Dad asked as we drove to the Emperor's house. He pulled a silver-wrapped candy out of the ashtray and popped it in his mouth, then handed one to me. The cab filled with the smell of Dad's butterscotch. I slipped mine in my pocket for Gayle.

"Sure," I said over the country song wailing out of the truck's speakers. "What kind of tree are we cutting?"

"Sycamore," he said. "It's a weed tree anyway, so it won't matter if you mess it up. The idiot"—by this he meant Mr. King—"had asked me to talk to Mrs. Cutlin about taking it out entirely, but he changed his mind yesterday." He spat out the window; a little of it flew back in the truck and landed on the dashboard. "Probably afraid it'd cost him more."

I didn't answer, just stared out my window, thinking about money, and the Emperor, and how poor everybody else in our town was.

Hilsabeck wasn't the smallest town in the county, but it shrank every year, with most of the young people leaving as soon as they could. It was all older folks' houses on the streets we took on the drive from our place to the Emperor's. The homes were mainly one-story, red or gray brick squares with plastic flowers in the yards, or birdbaths. There were two churches on the route, a Brookshire Brothers grocery store, and a feed store and tractor supply with a giant sign advertising a deer corn special "this week only." I laughed; it had said that for at least three years.

The air conditioner in the truck didn't work, so I kept my window down, soaking in the morning cool and the wild verbena–scented wind, until we got to the Emperor's. Dad got out and pointed to the sycamore he wanted trimmed. "That's today's job," he said. It was the one Gayle had built her nest in. *Good,* I thought. That tree was a menace.

Mr. King was waiting for us at his front door. His face was reddish, like he was out of breath. Or maybe it was just the reflection of light from the towering walls of red brick behind him. The two-story house was almost like the nicest ones in town, brick on all sides and a porch to sit on. Bigger, of course, and cleaner. He had a cleaning lady who did everything, even windows, or so Mom had heard. But the Emperor's house had tall white columns on the front porch that didn't go with the brick, and fancy white woodwork around all the windows. Like somebody had taken the front of a Southern plantation and plunked it on the front of a normal house. *No amount of cleaning could make all the parts match,* I thought. But it sure did make an impression.

The Emperor wasn't in his dressing gown today; he was wearing a three-piece suit, dark charcoal gray. Something flashed at his wrists as he raised a hand to greet us. Diamond cuff links, probably. I'd heard he even had diamond buttons on his tuxedo. "John," he said to my dad, and nodded. "Are you planning on working the south side today?"

Dad forced a smile and nodded back deeply—more or less bowing. "Yes, sir, Mr. King," he said. "That was the plan."

I couldn't watch. I swallowed and turned away, studying the small blue flowers that lined the path. They were perfectly placed, each one six inches from the next. *They'll be too close when they mature,* I thought. But the Emperor probably wouldn't have to worry about that. When they got too crowded, he'd just have his regular gardener dig them up and throw them out. Then they'd put in a batch of something else new and showy.

"Is there any chance I could borrow your son this morning?"

The Emperor's words drew my attention away from the flowers. "What?" I said before I could think better of it. "What for?"

My dad rested his hand on my arm and squeezed tight. I tried not to flinch; the Emperor was looking at me expectantly.

"I'm sorry, sir," my dad said. "I need his help to trim those sycamore branches."

"Oh, I'm sure you can do without him for a few hours." Mr. King's voice sounded happy, but his eyes were flat and hard. He was used to getting his way.

But my dad wasn't going to give up that easily. "It'll take longer," he said. "Cost more in the long run." He nodded once.

Mr. King waved a hand, flashing his diamond cuff links as he dismissed my dad like he was a waiter bringing a refill of water. "Not a problem."

Dad had never been able to hide his feelings. Of course, nobody had ever told him that—he was too quick-tempered. But his expression showed it all. Usually it was helpful; I knew when he was getting mad, so I could get out of arm's reach in time. But watching as he swallowed his anger, seeing humiliation parade across his face as his boss dismissed the prospect of extra money like it was a pile of dead leaves, I wished he could hide it. My own face burned as Mr. King's eyebrow twitched upward.

I think the man was trying not to smile.

He took a step and patted my dad on the shoulder, like they were friends. "Oh, come on, John. Trim that sycamore later. You still have some work on those pecans, and he'll be done soon enough. I just need him for a while."

"What for?" my dad said, echoing the same words I'd gotten in trouble for.

"Oh, some light gardening," Mr. King said as he shepherded my dad back toward the truck. "Snails in the bulb beds, that sort of thing."

Dad jerked his head once. "Fine." He walked off to our beat-up truck without looking at me, without saying anything.

I turned to Mr. King. "Sir? If you show me where the snails are—"

He cut me off. "There's plenty of time for that . . . John, isn't it? John, like your dad?"

"Yes, sir." He wanted something, I could see that. His eyes were shadowed and bloodshot, with tiny red veins stretching out from them like veins on a leaf. Dark circles, too, like he hadn't slept in a month. "Did you have something else for me to do?"

"A question, actually," he said. His eyes shifted back and forth, from me to the fence line where the sycamore stood, leaves rustling lightly. I waited for the question, but he didn't say anything, just stared at the spot on the fence.

Or right above it.

"About Gayle?" I asked after a few seconds.

"Who?" I had startled him, I think. He spun back to me, his lips tight, but he didn't look mad, just intense. "The girl who was singing, that's her name?"

"Gayle," I repeated. "Yeah."

"I thought . . . I heard it was something else. Tell me about her," Mr. King said. "What do you know?"

I had never seen a grown-up look the way Mr. King did when he asked about Gayle. His face shone like a kid who'd just seen a candy truck tip over on the highway.

Greedy.

I didn't like it. I took a step back. "Why don't you ask her yourself?"

"I tried," he said, still not looking at me. "I heard her singing this morning and went over. But she was frightened. She"—he laughed once, a soft huff of air—"she flew away."

Flew away. That's what Gayle had said about her parents. Had he heard everything Gayle and I had been talking about the day before? He was sure interested in that little girl . . . but he didn't look just interested. On his face was something . . . deeper.

A chill ran down my spine. I was glad Gayle had run off; this guy was definitely creepy. I took another step back.

"Well, ask Mrs. Cutlin, then."

He sighed. "I tried. She wasn't . . . receptive."

So even the nasty old Mrs. Cutlin had thought Mr. King's interest in Gayle was weird? Maybe she wasn't so bad after all.

Finally, he looked down at me. His face changed the instant he did—and as soon as he saw my expression he laughed. Not just laughed, he belly laughed, and sounded like Santa. "Oh, John, you should see the look on your face!" he managed after a few seconds. "Looking at me like I was planning to kidnap that little girl."

"Were you?" I tried not to sound as suspicious as I felt.

"No, of course not," he said. "Don't ever try to play poker, by the way. You're worse than your father, wearing every thought on your face. You'll lose your shirt."

I didn't say anything. My gut churned, though, at listening to him talk about my dad that way. Like he was pathetic. I felt ashamed of my own feelings from a few moments before.

Mr. King laughed a couple more times, then got control of himself, leaning against the stair rail. "It's commendable that you want to take care of her, though. Honorable."

"Thanks," I said. *Honorable?* That was a word I'd never heard used, at least not about me. And I still didn't know what he wanted. "About those snails . . ."

"Well, I'll admit, I didn't really want you to help with the garden." His lip twisted up on one side into a half smile. "I did want to talk to you about the girl. But not for any nefarious purpose."

"Why, then?" I didn't know what he meant by *nefarious*, but I still didn't trust him. This time, though, I tried not to show my feelings on my face. It must have worked, since he didn't smile. He looked serious and motioned me into the house. "Come with me. I want to show you something."

I'd never seen anything like his house. I don't think many people had; he never invited anyone over—not that my mom and her friends knew of, anyway. They gossiped about him a lot—about how much money he had, and why he lived alone in a little Podunk town like ours, in the middle of Mills County, and what he did locked up in that big house all day long.

I had a feeling I was about to find out. I opened my eyes as wide as I could and tried to remember what I was seeing, so I could tell Mom later. She'd love that.

It was so dark at first, though, and my eyes hadn't adjusted to the inside, that I missed a lot. I could tell there was wood paneling, dark wood like walnut or old cherry, and a few tables and chairs—carved ones—here and there in the front hall. No flowers, though, even if the gardens outside were full of them. No pictures hanging up that I could see, but there were—plates, it looked like. China. What kind of guy hung a bunch of dishes on the wall?

I remembered something my mom had said: The Emperor's Emporium stores had sold china plates first. Cheap ones that chipped the first time you used them. She'd gotten a set for a present when she got married, still had one plate that she used at Christmas to serve the cranberries.

The plates on Mr. King's walls looked fragile, sure. But not cheap. They looked like something you'd find in a museum. Delicate and expensive. You'd never touch them, that was for sure. "Woo-ee," I breathed. I stuffed my hands deeper in my pockets, the rustle of the candy wrapper shushing me.

As Mr. King led me down the hallway, our feet tapped on a floor that shone in the dim light like glass. It was marble, I saw, with some sort of inlaid pattern in blues and greens that made me think of foreign countries. It looked icy, almost, and it matched the cold air that jetted out from the AC vents high up on the walls. The chill reminded me of the principal's office at school; Ernest had always said the principal kept the temperature set to subarctic, so that the misbehaving kids were already trembling before he called them in.

I'd only been to the office once, for punching Jeb, but Ernest had been right about the cold, and the shivering. Maybe that was why I was shaking a little bit now, thinking about the principal.

"My study is this way," Mr. King said. He opened a sliding door, and I followed, feeling my feet sink into thick carpet at the doorway. It hardly seemed possible, but it was even colder in the study.

"This is what I want from your little friend," he said and motioned to something on the low table in the center of the room. I couldn't see what it was, but the gleam was back in his eye. It made my skin crawl. What was he pointing at? I took a step to the side and saw it at last, but I still didn't understand what I was looking at.

There were blinking lights and a microphone, a bunch of black boxes with dials and knobs. It looked like a combination of a computer and an old-fashioned radio. "What is it?" I asked after a few seconds.

Mr. King's eyebrows dipped, like he was disappointed in me. But then he tilted his head, thinking. "I suppose you could call it," he said at last, his voice going dreamy and soft, "a cage."

Chapter 4

"What the he—" The cuss almost slipped out as I backed away. This man was officially nuts, and I felt like getting the heck out of there, just in case it was the contagious kind of crazy. But I stopped myself. He wasn't threatening me. And if he was planning to do something against Gayle, I wanted to know exactly what. "What do you mean, a cage?"

Mr. King was fiddling with knobs and dials on the machine in front of him and didn't answer for a minute. While he worked, I looked around the room. There weren't any bars on the windows, just sheer curtains. But the walls? I'd never seen anything like it.

The walls were papered with music, sheets of music that looked like they were originals, not copies. Hanging in golden frames were dozens of pictures of singers—opera singers, I guessed, since I didn't recognize any of them, and they were all sort of fat and dressed in formal clothes. The pictures were all signed "Dear Emperor" or "To my favorite monarch." Things like that.

Was Mr. King a musician? I scanned the room for instruments—a piano or guitar or flute. But there wasn't anything in the room except one chair, the table with the machines, and shelves that were crammed with folders of some sort.

"What did you mean, a cage?" I asked again, when it seemed like Mr. King had completely forgotten I was there. But he just held up one finger and pushed a button. "Listen," he whispered, commanded. "Listen."

A woman's voice soared out of the machine. Well, not out of the machine exactly—it thundered out of the walls, crashing onto both of us like a tidal wave of sound. Where was it coming from? The walls, I realized. He had built-in speakers surrounding us, and the singing was pouring out of every wall. "Turn it down," I yelled, and covered my ears.

He stood there for a few seconds more, glorying in it, his face shining, eyes closed. Then he twisted a dial, and the music became bearable, less intense. "I love this part," he said, and motioned to the chair. "Sit down," he urged. "Listen. This note—the one that's coming—hear how she holds it, unfurls it, teases you with it, then draws it away. Ah! Magic. And I have it here, captured. Only for me."

I listened, but shook my head. I didn't hear all that, but I didn't want to say so. I just heard a woman singing opera. What I wanted to know was why he had called the machine a cage.

And what it had to do with Gayle.

I suppose he saw my expression and realized I wasn't really listening. He muttered a word that sounded like "philistine" and turned it off. My ears hummed with the leftover vibrations.

"Thanks," I said. "That was loud."

"I thought you kids liked loud music," he grumped, fiddling with his cuff links. "Rock music concerts and such."

"Yeah, well . . ." I said, trailing off. I didn't want to admit I wasn't like that. I hadn't spent much time with music at all, opera or rock. Music didn't matter that much to me.

Or it hadn't before I heard Gayle. "So, why did you say it was a cage?" I asked, trying to keep the suspicion out of my tone. "It's a music player, right?"

"And a recorder," he corrected, moving his hands over the controls again, as if he couldn't stop touching them. "I'm a collector, young John," he said, waving a hand at the black boxes. "But I don't collect stamps or"—his eyebrow quirked up—"worthless porcelain dolls from television advertisements."

I flushed, thinking about Mom's prized collection of Franklin Mint dolls that had sat in her closet until a few months back.

"I collect voices."

"How do you collect a voice?" I asked.

He smiled, like I'd asked the right question. "I've traveled across the world and recorded all of the great voices of our age—the most beautiful sounds any human has made for thirty years. I have them here." He motioned to the shelves. "Records first, then tape recordings, CDs. Now digital—it's wonderful, it catches every single vibration." He stood up and walked over to the wall. "It's only a cage for sound, but it's the perfect cage—all those voices, like birds in a personal aviary." He laughed—at himself, I thought. "And I've made this room into a studio, of sorts. I've embedded acoustic insulation, microphones as well."

"So, it's a recording studio?" I looked around. "Who are you going to record?"

His smile moved slowly across his face, spreading from his lips to his cheeks, then his glittering eyes. "That's the thing. I've been looking for the perfect voice for decades. And I think I've found it." His eyes darted to the window, in the direction of the Cutlins' house.

I had to warn Gayle about this nut job, and the sooner the better. "Look, Mr. King, I'm not certain what you want from me. I'll be happy to help you with your snails, or whatever, in your garden. But I can't help you with . . . this." I waved at his machine.

The smile dipped, and hardened. "I think you can," he said. "And I think you will. I'm not going to hurt that little girl, or you." He paused, and in that pause I heard the words he didn't say, the words we both knew. Even though he *could* hurt me, and her. Even though we couldn't do anything about it. And then he went on, "Or your father."

I tried not to gasp. I got it. He wouldn't hurt us . . . if I did what he wanted.

I stood up, right next to him, and took a quick step back. For the first time, I was aware of Mr. King's size. He was shorter than I was—five foot six, maybe. Not tiny, but I was bigger. It didn't make any difference, though. Even if I was bigger, he was stronger in all the ways that mattered. He could ruin my life, fire my dad. Mom was already having trouble finding food enough for the three of us on Dad's pay. And rent was due soon. If Mr. King fired him . . .

"What do you want?" I asked, trying to keep my voice from shaking, from anger or shame or fear, I didn't know. I had to get away before I did something, said something I shouldn't. I balled my hands up, stopping the trembling in my fingers.

"A small thing," the Emperor said. "I want you to ask your little friend to sing for me. Here, in my house. That's not hard, is it?"

I hesitated. What was the catch? "Just . . . sing?"

"Yes," he said. "Just a song. I want to record her voice. There's nothing wrong with that, is there?"

"No," I said slowly. "I guess not." I had a thought. "Why don't you just ask her yourself?"

"I've been trying to," he said, and laughed. "For some reason, every time she sees me coming, she runs off, or hides in that tree." He paused. "She's built a nest, hasn't she? Like a bird?"

"Yes," I said, remembering for an instant the softness of her hair. *I'd felt that same softness somewhere else,* I thought. Where had it been? Trying to remember, I almost didn't hear Mr. King's next words.

"—five hundred dollars, if you can get her to come inside in the next few days. Does that sound acceptable?"

"What?" He was talking about money? "Excuse me, I didn't hear that. *What* hundred?"

"Five hundred dollars," he repeated, moving slowly toward the door. I followed him, went through the opening and back into the hall of plates. "If you can convince that remarkable girl to sing her best for me, here."

Why was he offering to pay me? It felt wrong, like there was something he wasn't telling me. Five hundred dollars, though. That was as much as my dad was making in a week. With five hundred dollars, I could buy all sorts of things. A really good video game setup, like Ernest had, or an MP3 player. I could get Mom some new clothes, or take her to dinner. Heck, I could buy Dad a fishing rod, too. He had been a great fisherman when I was younger, bringing home giant catfish and bluegill most weekends for Mom to fry up. You never had to worry about going hungry, Dad had told me once, if you had a fishing rod.

Of course, he'd had to pawn his, right after the funeral. Too bad the funeral home man wouldn't take fish for payment, Dad had said.

People always said money couldn't buy happiness. Well, rich people said it. Me? I had been poor for a long time, and unhappy on top of that for the past ten months. I wasn't sure if money could buy happiness, but five hundred dollars? It was worth a shot. Still . . . I thought of Gayle, sitting up in her tree, the bruises on her arms. I didn't want her to get any more hurt.

Well, come on, Little John, I thought. *You're not going to let this man do anything.* Anything other than record her singing, if she'd let him. I was plenty taller than him, and if it came down to it, I could probably beat him. He had soft hands, small arms. He was weak, in the way only rich men could afford to be.

I remembered the feeling of Gayle in my arms, the lightness of her body and her smile. I'd protect her with my fists, if I had to.

Really, what could it hurt? Just a song. That was all he wanted.

"I'll ask her," I said at last. "She may not be home today."

"School doesn't start for weeks," he said. "And I heard her singing out there this morning." He paused, his hand on the front door handle. "It's amazing, isn't it? Her voice. Have you ever heard anything like it?"

"No," I said, remembering the way the sound had tried to lift me off the ground, into the sky. "Have you?"

"No." The Emperor's eyes glimmered as he whispered his answer so softly the closing door almost stole the word. "Never."

I walked blinking into the sunshine, and circled the house to see if I could convince Gayle to come down into the Emperor's cage.

Chapter 5

Gayle wasn't in her tree when I went to look, so I walked around the front of the Emperor's house and over to the Cutlins'. They lived in a one-story gray brick house that had been built long enough ago to need serious repairs. The mortar was coming out from between the bricks, and the brass work by the door was covered with black grime. The doorbell was broken, too, a sharp wire poking out where the button should be. *Nice,* I thought. *Really welcoming.*

The house was about the same size as our house, except ours was wood and vinyl siding. But at least Mom had kept ours nice-looking, with serious spring cleanings twice a year, up until last year. Maybe I could do the spring cleaning for her this summer. Clean the gutters and the sidewalks. That might make Mom happy. Maybe we could do it together, like we used to.

I shook the thought away. I was here to get Gayle, not daydream.

I stuck my hand through a fist-sized hole in the screen and knocked on the wooden front door as loud as I could. I heard someone yelling inside—"Jeb, stop her! It might be the case-worker!"—and footsteps running toward the door, so I pulled my hand out of the hole—not carefully enough. The rusted wire mesh scraped against the top of my hand and left a pattern of bleeding scratches across the tops of my knuckles.

"Dang it," I said, rubbing the scratched skin on the back of my jeans to wipe away the blood.

The door opened, and Gayle stood there, the cooler air from the hallway rushing out past her like it couldn't wait to be outside, and tangling her hair as it went.

Her hair was even messier today than the day before, if that was possible. My mom would have said it was full of birds' nests; she used to say that to Raelynn all the time, after we'd been playing in the fields all day. "A nest made out of burrs and beauty," Mom would complain as she brushed out my sister's golden-red hair.

Gayle smiled up at me, though I could see the tracks of old tears in the dirt on one of her cheeks.

"Hi, Tree," she whispered. I wanted to remind her not to call me that, but Jeb Cutlin appeared behind her, his hand raised up, like he was planning to grab her—or hit her. Gayle saw him coming and ducked instinctively.

I took a breath and reached for the screen door latch—if Jeb hit Gayle, I was going to have to remind him what being hit felt like—but he stopped in time. "Oh, hey, Little John." He put his hand on his hair like he was checking it, like he'd never been planning to do anything else with it.

Mrs. Cutlin's voice interrupted. "Who is it?" Her tone was sweet—just in case it was Gayle's caseworker, I guessed.

"It's just Little John Fischer," Jeb yelled back.

Her voice changed back to normal, harsh and grumpy. "What's he here for?"

Jeb turned back to me. "Yeah, what are you here for?"

"I wanted to talk to Gayle," I said.

"Who?" Jeb looked confused. "Who do you mean?"

Gayle had scooted away from the door, and she wouldn't look at me. "Her," I said, wondering what was going on.

"Oh, you mean Suzie? What for?" Jeb let out a hard laugh. "She told you her name was Gayle?" He turned to Gayle, who had wrapped her arms around herself tightly. "I thought Momma told you to stop calling yourself that. It ain't your name, Suzie." He rolled his eyes. "This one's a crazy. You know that, don't you?" he asked me. "Her real name's Suzie McGonigal. This is her third foster home in a year."

I looked down at Gayle. She was ignoring us as hard as she could. "Her third?"

"Yeah, she ran away from the others."

I gave Jeb a look. "Maybe she had a good reason to." If the other homes were anything like this one, I wouldn't have blamed her.

"Nah. First she said she had to go find her parents, right? But now she says her parents are birds, and they're going to fly here to find her. She even built a nest. We had to make her come down from that stupid tree last night." He opened the screen door and motioned me inside.

"No, thanks," I said. "Can you send her on out? Or are you afraid she'll run away again?"

"You kidding? We're so far out here, they figure there's no-where to run, right? That's probably the only reason they let Mom have another foster anyhow—" He stopped suddenly, like his brain had just then caught up with his mouth, and flushed red. "What do ya want with her?" Jeb darted a glance at Gayle again. "She do something wrong?"

What was I going to tell him? That the Emperor had asked her to come sing? That I wanted to earn five hundred dollars? I remembered Verlie Cutlin's voice the day before, calling Gayle's music "racket." *I'd better not mention it,* I thought. Proba-bly it would get her into even more trouble. I had an idea.

"Nah," I said, "My mom wanted to know how old she was, some other stuff. She's putting together some school supplies for all the foster kids." That was partly true; Mom did a drive every year for all the "unfortunates," as she called them. "She said to ask if she needed a backpack, her favorite color. That kind of stuff."

I shouldn't have bothered to go on. Jeb's attention had been drawn away by the blaring of a sports game from the television. Probably baseball, I thought, or maybe preseason football. For a second I wanted to go in and watch. I hadn't been able to see the good games on ESPN for months. We had a television, but no money for cable.

It was my own fault, really. I could have gone next door and watched with Ernest; last year, we'd taken turns at his house and ours watching the whole Major League Baseball season. It was supposed to be our new tradition. But I hadn't wanted to tell Ernest how bad things had gotten at my house, so I'd told him I didn't like baseball anymore. That I'd outgrown it, just like video games.

I'd outgrown almost everything that cost money, it turned out, since we'd had to spend all of Mom's savings on a four-foot-long pine box and a burial plot.

Jeb nodded. "Just keep an eye on her—Mom says she has to have a bath before the caseworker gets here. Don't let her fly away or nothing." He laughed like he'd made a joke, but it didn't make me smile. It just made me want to punch him.

"Thanks, Tree," Gayle whispered when we'd stepped outside and Jeb had slammed the door behind us.

"Don't call me that," I said. "And what's the deal? Suzie? Your name isn't Gayle?"

"It is," she insisted. But she snuck a look back at the door to make sure it was closed, and ran a few steps away, around to the side yard. Once we were out of sight of the door, she started skipping and windmilling her arms. "Come on, slowpoke," she called, and ran through the broken chain-link gate into the backyard. I followed, sighing. I'd seen my sister in this mood before. Hyper, like a kid who had sat in church too long.

There wouldn't be any explaining, or asking about visits to the Emperor's, until she'd run around a bit. I almost couldn't remember feeling that way. Like a kid.

The Cutlins' yard was huge, at least three acres. It was surrounded by a run-down chain-link fence on all the sides except the Emperor's; he'd paid to have a tall wooden fence put up there. I'm sure he was trying to avoid having to look at their old house, even though he still must've been able to see it, what with his own house being up on a rise.

The Cutlins' land itself was boggy, and mosquitoes buzzed in low-lying clouds near the squishy parts of the lawn in the evenings and late afternoons. But right now, it was ten in the morning, and the sunlight hit the wet places and turned the water on the grass into crystals that spun into the air as Gayle ran past.

Or whatever her name was.

I caught up to her on the far side of the property, near the base of an old pecan tree. Last season's nuts and shells crunched under my feet as I approached, and Gayle heard me coming and looked up. I hadn't noticed in the house—I guess it had been too dark—but she had a red mark on one of her cheeks.

I leaned down and brushed my hand against her face. "Did Jeb do that?"

She shook her head but didn't add anything more. She plucked a dandelion near her feet and hunkered down, blowing until all the fluff drifted away, sparkling in the sunlight.

"Who, then?"

She shrugged. "It was an accident," she said after a few seconds and another dandelion. "I didn't mean to."

"Didn't mean to what?" I tried to make my voice as soft as I could, even though the hard knot of anger in my belly made the words sound rougher than I intended.

Gayle leaned against me, and I felt her hair brush my arm. I reached down and petted her, my hand stroking once, twice, the way my mom used to do when I was little. The way she hadn't done in almost a year.

But Momma had told me I was the size of a man now, and I should expect to be treated like one.

I was glad to be so much stronger, most of the time. My muscles were harder, and so were the calluses on my hands from helping my dad with the business. It was just . . . I didn't know getting big meant the end of *anything* soft. Maybe if Raelynn hadn't died, I'd still have one person who would hug me.

Gayle leaned in closer and said, "I'm not supposed to sing. But Mrs. Cutlin hurt herself on the stove, and I thought if I sang, it would help her. But . . . it didn't."

I wasn't sure what Gayle meant—that she thought her singing would help. Maybe she imagined it would cheer Mrs. Cutlin up. I could have told her that wouldn't work. Just last year, the woman had refused to let two other foster boys attend their own fifth-grade graduation swim party. She said they'd been acting up, and she wasn't going to reward bad behavior.

I remembered Jeb's slip of the tongue and wondered. Maybe the foster people knew Mrs. Cutlin wasn't all that nice. Maybe something *had* happened with those two boys. Maybe Mrs. Cutlin—or Jeb—had marked them up and didn't want anyone to see the signs of a beating. Gayle's face had grown so sad and closed off, I knew it was time to change the subject. But first . . . "Gayle? Why did Jeb say your name was Suzie?"

"That's what they call me," she said and shrugged. She pulled three pieces of tall Johnson grass up and began to braid them together, winding blossoms from the pink evening primroses that sprinkled the lawn into the braid. "But it's not my real name. I just pretend, so they'll leave me alone. Sometimes I forget."

"What is your real name?" I paused. Maybe Susan was her middle name, or something. "Your whole name, I mean."

"I'm not supposed to tell," she whispered. "That's what got me in the most trouble yesterday, when the preacher came with the extra clothes." She looked down and picked at the shirt she had on. It was a different shirt, I noticed, red and blue striped.

Not nearly as worn out as the one from yesterday, even if this one didn't fit her as well. "First he told Mrs. Cutlin I shouldn't be so dirty. He's the one who called the caseworker to come out today. Then he asked my name, and Mrs. Cutlin got so mad."

"Why?"

Gayle shrugged again, and ran over to the base of the sycamore. "She says if I act crazy, I'll have to live somewhere worse. She said to keep my mouth shut."

I knew why Mrs. Cutlin didn't want Gayle to act crazy. If she did, they might take her away and make Mrs. Cutlin foster some other kid, a bigger one that ate more, maybe even one she couldn't shove around. Or they might not let her foster any kids at all, and then how would she pay the cable bill?

"Come on," I said, standing up and pulling stray dandelion fluff off my shirt. "You can tell me your name. I won't say anything."

"I'll give you a hint," she said. Then she opened her mouth and sang. It sounded like birdsong, almost exactly, but some kind of bird I'd never heard before. I could tell the difference between dozens of calls—cardinals to crows, meadowlarks to mourning doves. But this? It was more beautiful than any bird I'd ever heard.

"Well," she said, her eyes shining. "Can you guess my name now?"

Guess her name from a birdsong—one I didn't even recognize? I felt like I had in sixth grade math, when Mrs. Clark would call on me even though she knew I didn't know the answer. I rubbed the back of my hand against my face to wipe away a bead of sweat. "I don't know," I said. "Sorry."

She shook her head, the light fading in her eyes slightly. "Fine. I'll tell you. But you have to promise not to tell anyone else, okay? If Mrs. Cutlin found out . . ." Her voice trailed off again, and she touched the red spot on her cheek lightly.

"I won't tell," I said, and meant it. What I didn't say was that I had decided to tell my mom—maybe even my dad—about Mrs. Cutlin. There had to be something we could do to help Gayle out. To get her away from the Cutlins, at least some of the time.

Even though I promised, she looked worried. I'd seen that expression on my mom's face before, when the landlord came to talk about late rent, but I'd never seen a kid look like that. Like she had all the weight of the world on her.

I wished there was something I could do to get rid of that anxious shadow behind her eyes. Then I remembered the candy in my pocket. "Oh. I brought this for you." She nodded, smiled a little, and took the butterscotch, fiddling with the silver wrapper.

"Okay," she said at last, like the candy had decided for her. "It's a nightingale's song. My mom told me it was the most beautiful sound in the world. That's my name. Nightingale."

"Nightingale?" I repeated as she unwrapped the candy and

popped it into her mouth. Who named their kid Nightingale? I wondered what kind of parents she had had, and what had happened to them. A car accident? Of course, the kind of people who named their kid Nightingale probably didn't own a car. It was sort of a hippie name; at least that's what my dad would say. But I liked it. It suited her. "That's a beautiful na— Hey, stop it!" She had started to climb the sycamore tree, one-handed, toward her nest, carrying her braided-grass crown between her teeth, and her candy wrapper like a treasure in her right hand. I had never seen anyone climb a tree so fast; she was like one of those wrens perching sideways, hopping from one branch to the next on her way up the tree, almost too fast to see how she held on. Watching, I felt sick, like I might throw up.

"Gayle!" I yelled, a little louder. "Get down from there!"

She must have figured out I was serious. She stopped and looked down at me. "Why?" she said, her head cocked to the side, burred lumps of hair swinging out as she did. "Aren't you going to come up, too?"

Come up? I would have laughed, but I felt so queasy, I held my mouth shut. I took a few deep breaths, feeling the sick, clammy sweat gather on my neck. "I don't climb trees," I said finally, looking away, toward the Emperor's house, and remembered the reason I was here in the first place. "Let's do something else."

"Little John," she complained. For the first time since I'd met her, her voice didn't sound like a silver bell. Her little-kid whining almost made me smile. "You gotta come up. There's something I want to show you."

"Well, bring it down here," I said roughly. "I don't have all day, you know. I have to go do some work next door."

"Work?" she repeated. "What kind of work?"

"Well, I gotta pick snails for a bit. I'm supposed to be helping Dad with a couple of old pecans over at Mr. King's," I said, wondering if I could work the conversation around to her singing for him, possibly.

"Oh!" She almost fell off the side of the tree in her excitement. "You're taking care of his trees?"

I chuckled. "More like taking them out. We're supposed to cut down two this week, and trim up the rest."

She was silent. "You're going to cut them . . . down?" I looked up; there was true horror in her voice.

"Yeah," I said. "Dad says I'm big enough to do it myself—with him helping, sure. But he thinks I'm old enough." I flexed a muscle. "And strong enough."

"Don't do it, please, Little John," she said, clambering down from the tree at last. "I love the trees here. They're . . . they're the only things I can trust."

"Trust?" I said, trying not to laugh. "Trees?" I shook my head. "Listen, Gayle. Trees are just wood that hasn't been cut down yet. Old ones like those pecans at Mr. King's are a hazard—the limbs get rotten, and then they're dangerous."

"Trees aren't dangerous," she said, like I was dumb. It made me mad.

"I know what I'm talking about," I said, louder. "I knew a little girl who fell out of a tree no bigger than that stupid one you built your nest in. It's not safe." I let out my breath and walked a few steps toward the fence.

Behind me, Gayle was silent. And then I heard a soft word and felt an even softer hand on my arm. "Who?"

I knew what she meant. "My sister," I said, feeling the back of my throat start to burn. I swallowed hard. There was no use crying; Dad had told me as much fifty times in the last ten months. No use crying now, when there was nothing to be done.

"I'm sorry," Gayle said. She inched her fingers down my arm and held my hand, lightly brushing the scratches I'd gotten from the Cutlins' screen door. "Here," she said. "You're hurt. Shut your eyes and let me sing you better."

It was cute, I thought. She wanted to sing me a song to make me feel better. I hadn't even asked her yet about singing for the Emperor, but I could wait a few minutes. Humor her. I heard the Emperor's back door open, way off on the other side of the fence. Was he going in or coming out? I wasn't quite tall enough to see that far over. "Go ahead, then," I said, and shut my eyes.

The first notes that came out were sad, almost cries. I squeezed my eyes shut even tighter as I realized she wasn't singing birdsong now. It was just as high, but the notes were more . . .

purposeful. More meaningful, it seemed like. She still didn't use words, but the melody was the thing—her voice sailed and looped, like a swallow, up and over the sadness that had lodged in my throat, around my heart, loosening the tightness there, too, and even down my arms and into my hands.

My fingers tingled for a moment. I cracked my eyes open when I heard the flutter of wings. A dozen or so grackles had taken up position on the fence, heads cocked, listening intently. They didn't make a single sound—something I'd never realized grackles were capable of, the noisy things. And then, when the song changed, turned into a light melody and ended, the last few notes spiraling like pollen on a breeze, the grackles all nodded and flew away together.

"That was the strangest thing," I said. "I've never seen—"

"Is it better now?" I heard. I thought she was asking if I felt better, and I nodded. But she made an impatient *tsk* and reached for my arm again. "Little John, you didn't even check."

I realized then she was examining the bloody scrape marks on my hand. What was she looking for? "It's okay," I said. "It'll be better in a week."

"No," she said, and a smile beamed out. "It's better now." And she lifted up my hand.

The scratch marks were almost gone.

Chapter 6

"All better?" She had asked it twice, but I hadn't been able to answer.

Not even able to think, really. I just stared at my hand, wiping the few remaining dried flecks of blood off the skin. The pale scratches underneath looked old—days old. I couldn't believe it.

I *didn't* believe it. It had to be my imagination. I couldn't have scratched it very bad in the first place, right?

But I knew it had been bleeding. My jeans had rusty streaks on them where I'd wiped the cut.

I held my hand up to my mouth and licked it, to be sure. The faint taste of iron and salt drifted across my tongue.

"Gayle?" I asked at last, looking down at her. She wouldn't look at me now, though.

"Was it okay, Little John?" she asked, her voice a whisper as soft as the breeze that rustled the Johnson grass. "Did I heal it good?"

"Yeah," I said, clearing my throat. "Yeah, it's fine." So . . . she thought she'd healed it, too? If we both thought that, could it be our imaginations?

Or was it real?

My head buzzed, and I wondered if I was going to hyper-ventilate. Maybe I'd been out in the heat too long. That would explain it. I decided to play along, though. "I'm fine. Thanks, Gayle," I said after a few more seconds. I sat down, the seat of my pants crushing a few dandelions. She hunkered down next to me, her arms resting lightly on her knees. Timid, almost, like a wren that might hop away at my slightest movement. I reached one hand out and ruffled her hair again. "It's okay," I said. "So, how did you learn to sing so good?"

"The healing song?" she asked. I nodded, and tried to keep my heart from thumping out of my chest. She really did think she'd done something.

Maybe she had. I ignored the pulsing of the blood through my hand.

"You won't tell?" she said. "My mom and dad said I wasn't ever to tell, except the trees, of course." She said it so matter-of-factly, I couldn't help but nod.

"Of course." I swallowed, hard. "So . . . you can heal stuff. By singing?"

She nodded, then shook her head. "Well, some. I'm not

really good at it. My mom was, though. She could sing just about anything and make it all better. I can only do small things."

"Like a cut?"

She nodded and showed her even teeth in a proud smile. "Yep."

"Cool," I said at last. Then we both got quiet. I could hear the whine of my dad's chain saw across the fence. How long had I been over here? No more than ten minutes, probably. He wouldn't miss me yet. Behind me, from the Cutlins' house, I heard a raised voice. "Where's that girl?"

Dad might not miss me, but Mrs. Cutlin was already missing Gayle. When Gayle heard the woman's voice, though, she clambered up the tree before I could even grab her leg—and I tried, missing, and re-scraping my hand on the rough bark. I swore, softly so Mrs. Cutlin wouldn't hear, and called up to Gayle just as softly. "Get down here!" I hadn't even had a chance to ask if she would come across the fence and sing for Mr. King. The thought of the five hundred dollars, and all the things I could buy with that much money, made me feel itchy. I didn't have time to play pretend games with a little girl. I spoke louder. "You got to get down," I demanded. "Now!"

"No," a sulky voice called back to me. "She's mean. And you sound mean now, too. I'm staying in my nest."

I sighed. I wished Ernest were here. He had a way of getting Isabelle to do what he wanted without letting on that he was leading her. He'd know exactly what to say, what to do, to get Gayle down. Then I remembered a time when Ernest had been trying to get his sister to walk faster to school. It was her first week of kindergarten, and she'd decided she was sick and tired of the whole mess after only four days. She'd started walking slower and slower, until Ernest told Isabelle he was going to walk with Raelynn instead. Isabelle had practically run to keep up with us after that.

Maybe something like that would work. "Fine," I said, walking a few steps away, but slowly, looking over my shoulder as I went. "I was going to ask if you wanted to come over next door and help me in Mr. King's gardens. It's a paying job, and I was gonna ask Mrs. Cutlin if you could help me. But since you don't want to, I'll just ask Jeb."

Of course, there was no way I was going to ask Jeb Cutlin to do anything—other than jump off a cliff or hold still so I could beat him with my fists—but she didn't know that.

Thinking about it, I realized it was sort of dishonest, trying to get Gayle to do what I wanted by acting like I didn't care what she did. It felt bad, like I was tricking her. Lying, in a way.

It was all for a good cause, I told myself. Sure, I might get some money out of it. But Gayle would get to be away from the Cutlins. That was just as important, right?

But five hundred dollars was an awful lot of important, too.

My stomach flip-flopped. I hated feeling guilty—my stomach was the first part of me to start squirming. The sensation reminded me of the time I got food poisoning from the school cafeteria's sloppy joes and threw up for three days straight.

I was about to turn around, confess, when I heard "Wait!" behind me. It had worked.

I walked a little faster. There was a sound of twigs and bark scattering on the leaf mulch beneath the tree. I tried not to think of how high she'd been, or how fast she was coming down. As long as I didn't look back, I could keep calm enough. "Wait up, Tr— Little John!" she yelled.

A second later, I felt a hot hand slip into mine. I curled my fingers around hers and walked up to the Cutlins' front door. This time, I knocked on the wood of the screen door, avoiding the rusted wire. The door opened in a flash, and I had a feeling Mrs. Cutlin had been about to come out looking for Gayle— she had a hard, set expression on her face, the kind my mom used to get when it was time for spring cleaning. Not happy, but determined. Gayle hid behind me as we spoke.

"Good morning, Mrs. Cutlin," I said. "I hope you don't mind, but I have a favor to ask."

The wrinkles on the sides of Mrs. Cutlin's mouth got deeper and deeper as I explained that Mr. King wanted me to do some gardening.

"What can a kid your age do?" she started, then stopped as I straightened up and she saw how tall I was. She shook her head, like I'd disappointed her by having a growth spurt. "Well, I don't see why you want Suzie."

"The petunia beds need some work," I lied. Mr. King's regular gardener was off for a couple of weeks, sure, but he'd left everything in pristine condition. But Mrs. Cutlin didn't need to know that. "There's a huge infestation of snails, and some weeding. I'm supposed to help my dad with the trees," I explained, and flexed my arm slightly so she could see the muscles there, see I wasn't just hanging around. "I'm needed on the big jobs. But Mr. King wants the garden done, too. So I wondered if Ga— I mean, if Suzie could help out. I'd pay her," I went on, when it looked like Mrs. Cutlin was about to start shaking her head *no*. "It's not much, just a couple of dollars a day, but it's better than nothing."

"The social worker's not coming until four," she said—to herself, I thought. Not thirty seconds later, we were standing outside the shut door, Mrs. Cutlin's admonition to "bring that money home, girl, and give it to me" still ringing in the warm morning air.

"You did it," Gayle whispered. "You escaped me."

"Sure thing. Let's go, jailbird," I teased, hearing the chain saw cut out for the first time in a while. "I really do have to help my dad."

And get Gayle into Mr. King's recording studio, I thought, the

59

idea churning up my stomach like those rotten sloppy joes. Good thing I'd only had toast for breakfast.

Maybe I was just hungry, I decided. "Let's get a snack on the way." We ran, laughing at everything and nothing, around the front of Mr. King's house.

Of course, when we got to the truck, my dad was waiting. And the look on his face made Mrs. Cutlin seem positively cheerful.

Chapter 7

"Where have you been, boy?" Dad's hand twitched on the door handle. I could tell he wanted to smack me, but then his gaze fell on Gayle. His eyes got big and he blinked twice, like he was trying to clear them. I thought I knew why: The last time I'd been running around holding hands with a little girl, it had been my sister. Gayle didn't look anything like Raelynn had, except for being about the same height. But they both had that same way of running, fast and carefree, like their feet were about to leave the ground. "Who's this?"

I took advantage of Dad's distraction to glance toward the house. Was Mr. King in there, watching? Did he think I'd brought Gayle over to sing for him?

"This is the Cutlins' new foster kid," I explained. "I thought she could help with the gardening."

"No," he said, and turned away.

"Dad, please."

He swung around, and his lips were tight. "I said no. Now get the Mickey Mouse garden work done and then get your tail out there. I got eighty more acres of pecans and only one of me. I need a hand."

"It'll get done quicker if she helps," I argued, wondering if I'd pushed it too far.

He answered in a soft growl. "We need every dime from this job. Send her home." I wished I could make Gayle go somewhere else to play for a few minutes. Just far enough that I could get Dad alone and tell him about the Cutlins and those marks on Gayle's arms. All my suspicions. But I didn't have to say anything. Mr. King took care of that.

The front door opened, and the Emperor stepped out, still dressed in his fancy clothes. "Oh, hello! Good job, Little John. You brought Gayle back with you! Wonderful."

I wanted to tell him that she hadn't come over to sing, not yet anyway, but Dad was looking at me strangely. "He asked you to get her?"

"Well, sort of," I said. I would have said more, but my tongue felt thick in my mouth. Besides, Gayle was clinging so tightly to my leg that I was starting to lose circulation in my foot. It was peculiar; the closer Mr. King got, the higher Gayle tried to climb up my leg that I leaned down. "What's wrong, Gayle?

It's only Mr. King." She didn't answer, just tucked her face into my jeans leg and shook her head.

By the time Mr. King reached us, her whole body was trembling.

I guess he must have noticed, because he didn't try to talk to her. He did turn to my dad, though. "Oh, John, I need to ask about what you're planning to do with the wood from those pecans. There's a company owned by an acquaintance of mine that makes amazing furniture out of burled pecan. Can you spare a minute, look at his website? I'm not certain those trees would be big enough."

Even though he was asking a question, the tone of his voice made it clear he expected Dad to stop work and go inside the house to talk about furniture. I stepped back, dragging Gayle through the dirt—it was entirely possible Dad would explode at Mr. King and tell him exactly where to stuff his burled pecan website.

But he didn't. Dad just nodded, mouth tight shut, and followed Mr. King up to the porch. He didn't say a word to me or Gayle, almost like he'd forgotten we were there.

"Gayle?" I whispered when they had gone. "What's the deal? Get off my leg, you silly goose."

She let go a little, and laughed once. "I'm not a goose. I'm a nightingale."

"You're a nutball," I said, and ruffled her hair. "Why does

Mr. King freak you out?" She wouldn't answer, just drew circles in the mulch with her toe.

"Is it because he smells like mothballs and pee?"

She couldn't hide her laugh. "No."

"Why, then?"

"When he talks to me, it sounds like . . ." she started, then let go of my leg and picked at a pebble by her foot.

"What?" I said, and leaned down, tipping her chin up so I could see her eyes. "What does it sound like when he talks to you?"

"Like a crow," she said at last. "It sounds like a crow feels."

I took a breath, wondering what in the world she meant— crows were loud, right? But she hadn't said it sounded like a crow *sounds*. "How does a crow feel?" I wanted to ask. How would anyone even know that? But Gayle had spotted a butterfly, and she was chasing the fluttering scrap of orange toward the back of the house.

Good, I thought. That's where the snails were, anyway. If there were any. I'd ask her about the crow thing later.

I just hoped it didn't mean she wouldn't sing for him. Crow or not, five hundred dollars could buy a lot of birdseed.

Turns out there *were* snails in the garden. So many that Gayle and I spent the rest of the day picking them off the soft leaves of Mr. King's flowers and flicking them toward the robins and jays that waited in the bushes, twittering and chirping so loud I almost didn't hear Dad when it was time to go.

"You gotta scoot," I said to Gayle, starting back toward the house. "Oh, wait. Money." Mrs. Cutlin would expect Gayle to have some money. I ran to the truck, with a yelled "Just a minute!" to Dad, who was settling up with Mr. King for the week. The glove compartment usually had a few dollars in it.

This time, though, it only had a few quarters and some other loose change. I scooped it all up and ran back to Gayle. It would have to do. "Here," I said. "Give this to Mrs. Cutlin. I'll bring some bills on Monday."

"Monday," Gayle repeated, holding the coins tightly, like they might vanish if they hit the ground. "Not till Monday?"

"I can't," I said. "I live on the other side of town."

"Gayle?" A soft voice came from behind her. I startled. It was Mr. King—he'd moved so quietly, neither of us had heard him. "Do you have time to sing for me today?"

Gayle made a choking sound. "Sing?"

"Yes, sing insi—" Mr. King said, and shot a look at me. I tried to tell him to shut up with my eyes, and he must have gotten it, because he stopped mid-word, and frowned. Then he looked back at Gayle. "Don't worry about it. My mistake." He reached a hand toward her, though, like he was going to pet her, or grab her, or something.

She was gone before he could finish the movement.

Together we watched her scamper across the grass and practically fly over the fence, scurrying up the tree and into her nest. I sighed; I'd seen most of the coins go flying, and I knew Mrs. Cutlin wouldn't be happy.

"Let's go, Little John," I heard Dad say, as the truck engine started up. Mr. King had a hand on my arm, though, and I looked down into his angry brown eyes.

"What's your game?" he said.

"No game, sir," I answered slowly, wondering what I should say. I decided on the truth. "I didn't have time to even ask her today. She's a little—scatterbrained. And she won't say anything around the Cutlins. I was just about to ask her when you came out. Give me some time."

"How much time?"

"Just a week," I said. I could probably convince Mrs. Cutlin that Gayle was needed for a week's worth of gardening. "I'll bring her over to work in your garden. Get her used to it." He looked doubtful, so I smiled. "You said it yourself. She's a scared little thing. Look at her now, hiding in a nest. She's like a bird. You got to move slow."

Finally, he nodded. "All right," he muttered. "A week. By next Friday, though." My relief must have showed on my face, because he squeezed my arm, a little harder than was friendly. "Listen," he said, "I'm dead serious about paying you to get that little girl to sing for me. But don't try to trick me. You'll regret it."

"No, sir," I promised, hearing my dad rev the truck engine. "I wouldn't do that."

He let go, and I ran for the truck, feeling his eyes on me the whole time, wondering again what Gayle had meant about his voice feeling like a crow's. I didn't get that—his voice sounded normal to me. But his eyes? They reminded me of a crow, for sure.

Weren't crows always pecking dead things in the road? Right then, I could feel his gaze stabbing into my back like a sharp beak, threatening worse if I didn't do what he asked.

Chapter 8

That night, I tried to talk to Mom about Gayle. I shouldn't have bothered; it was one of her bad nights. When I got home, she was sitting in Raelynn's room, going through her chest of drawers. The cat was in there with her, but it ran out when I came in. It had really been Raelynn's pet, not mine. It still slept in her room most nights.

"What are you doing, Mom?" I asked, soft so I wouldn't startle her. I couldn't see her face at first, so I didn't know if she'd been crying.

"Just making sure her things are all still nice," Mom said after a long enough pause that I wasn't sure she'd heard me in the first place.

"Nobody's been in here," I said. "It's all just like it should be."

"Shut up," Mom said, turning even further from me. "You shut up talking like that."

"What?" Mom never said *shut up*. I wasn't even allowed to say it in front of her, unless I wanted a slapped face. Mom thought it sounded tacky. What had I said that had set her off, made her forget her own rule? Then I realized. I'd told her everything was like it should be. "I didn't mean it that way, Mom. I just meant . . . nobody's touched anything."

Mom held up a handful of ribbons. The light filtered in through the dusty window, and made the glittery pink ones shine. Pink had been Raelynn's favorite, but she'd had hair ribbons in every color. Mom had French-braided them into her hair every day for school. I didn't think it was so much that Mom cared what her daughter's hair looked like. I think she'd done it just so she could feel it. Raelynn's hair had been reddish-yellow and superfine, like a baby's.

Mom set the ribbons back into the top drawer and slid it shut. "Go set the table, would you?" she said. "I need a moment."

I should have gone. But I'd spent the whole day being put off talking about what I'd wanted to say, so I kept at it. "Mom," I said, leaning against the doorframe. "I need to talk to you about Gayle."

Mom didn't speak, so I went on. "I think she's not being taken care of. I think . . . I think she's getting beat on some. By Jeb, and maybe even Mrs. Cutlin. She has marks on her face."

"She always has marks on her face," Mom said, her voice far away and dreamy. She laughed. "Never can eat an ice cream without dripping on her chin and her shirt, too. I swear that girl is worth her weight in laundry powder."

It was no use. She was talking about Raelynn again. I turned to go, but Mom's voice stopped me.

"Little John, you take care of her now, you hear? Those boys at school give her any trouble, you pop 'em, right in the mouth. I won't let your daddy punish you for fighting. You keep her safe."

She still meant Raelynn. Mom and I both knew I hadn't been able to keep my sister safe. Well, Mom knew it on her good days. But I was thinking about Gayle. I could take care of her. And I would.

"I will, Momma," I promised as I left, still remembering Gayle and the red mark on her cheek. I had to figure out a way to get her safe. "I'll take care of her."

I went out to set the table, hoping Mom would come out of Raelynn's room before Dad got back from the store. Hoping Dad wouldn't spend all the week's money on beer, too. Rent was due next Friday, and from what Mom said, that week's paycheck, added to her savings, would barely cover it.

Of course, I should have learned not to hope by now. Dad came home with a twelve-pack, three steaks, and three bottles of Jack Daniels. I never knew steak could taste like ashes. But with Mom crying at the wasted money, and Dad ignoring us, hammering back the beers in front of the stupid TV that barely had any channels anyway, I knew it didn't matter what we ate. It would all taste ruined, anyway.

Dad stayed drunk most of Saturday. Mom locked herself in her room, coming out every so often to scream at Dad about money. He yelled back. I knew everyone on our street could hear them; the windows were open to let in a breeze. I went to my room and stuck a chair in front of the door. Most of the day, I stayed on my bed reading one of my Audubon books out loud, trying to drown out the sounds of them crying and fighting, and looking for a picture of a nightingale. But I only had North American birds, and there weren't any nightingales that I could tell.

At church on Sunday, I sat next to Mom. Dad never came with us anymore. He was still sleeping off the booze, anyway.

I heard a shushing noise behind me about halfway through the prayer of confession. Mom had her head tucked low, praying as hard as she could for something. Probably for Dad to sober up. I opened my eyes and peeked back. It was Isabelle, sneaking away from her family, not very quietly. She tiptoed into my pew and sat right next to me. I peeked behind me at Ernest; he rolled his eyes and shrugged. I smiled and shrugged back. Isabelle was like a force of nature; there was no trying to hold her back when she decided on something.

When we stood up for the next hymn, Isabelle yanked on my arm. I leaned down, pretending to sing. "What?"

"You missed the funeral," she said, her eyes wide as ever.

"What funeral?" Then I remembered the bird. "For the chick?"

"Yes. It was beautiful. We dug the biggest hole you ever saw, with rocks on top so the cat wouldn't be able to dig it back up, and we had fourteen hymns and a eulogy longer than Pastor's sermons! And," she paused, then continued more softly when my mom shot her a look, "we made a casserole for the bereaved." She pulled the last word out long and low, like it was a magic spell.

"A casserole? For the birds?"

"Yes." She giggled. "Out of night crawlers and dead crickets all mashed up! It was awesome."

Next to us, my mom cleared her throat, so we both waited until Pastor Martin had gotten into his sermon—to one of the loud, shouting parts—to whisper again.

"Why didn't you stay?" Isabelle said, so soft I almost couldn't hear. "We missed you. Ernest misses you."

"Couldn't," I answered. "I had to work."

"But," she said, then stopped. She swung her white patent leather shoe back and forth under the wooden pew for a few seconds, then went on. "But you're just a kid. Why do you got to work?"

I knew the answer to that, even if I wasn't going to say it out loud. I thought about it all through the sermon, though, even while I was playing hangman on the side of the bulletin with Isabelle.

I'd heard enough women gossiping in the fellowship hall after services, talking about my dad and the rotten oak he'd let stand. Raelynn's oak. I knew the church people blamed Dad for Raelynn's death.

I was glad they didn't know it was really my fault. That's why I worked so hard. I had to try and make up for what I'd done to the family, my family. Even though I never could fix it.

I peeked up at the big wooden cross at the front of the sanctuary. My dad had cut down the tree for the wood the year I was born. It was maple, with a burled pattern near the top that looked a little like the face of Jesus, if you stared hard enough.

I stared at it now, wondering for the millionth time why God would let Raelynn die.

And then, why a kid like Gayle had so many bad things in her life. It wasn't right.

I didn't know if I believed in prayer, but I squeezed my eyes shut and said one anyway, for Gayle, and that I would be able to find some way to get her away from the Cutlins, for a few hours at least. Which was going to be hard, considering I'd need some money to pay her with, and I had exactly twenty cents to my name.

I had just finished my prayer when the minister called the ushers up for the offering plates.

Mom always told me God answered prayer. I never thought He would be so quick about it, though. I mean, that had to be it, right? The offering plate passed in front of us, right at the very minute Isabelle's mom had obviously had enough of her daughter's loud whispers, and walked up the aisle to retrieve her. Isabelle jumped up so quick—as she should have, what with the look in her mom's eyes promising all sorts of spankings if she didn't hop to it—that she knocked against the plate, and a bunch of bills flew out. I picked all of them up, I thought, and passed the plate on.

But then, a few seconds later, I saw one that had flown under my feet. A ten-dollar bill. I looked around. Had no one else noticed? Mom was praying hard, her eyes shut. The usher was waiting for Mrs. Herrington to tear a check out of her checkbook. The organist was playing almost as loud as my heart was beating. All I had to do was move my shoe over the bill and not look down, not draw any attention to it.

Guilt twisted at me. The money was for the needy, I knew. But Gayle was the neediest kid in town, right? So I said to heck with guilt, and slipped the bill in my pocket after the prayer of thanksgiving.

"Thanks," I whispered to the cross. "I'll use it right."

Chapter 9

That Monday, Dad was still so hungover when we got to the Emperor's, he didn't even complain when I ran off to get Gayle. Mrs. Cutlin answered the door, her hair hanging all down her face. She hadn't bothered to put any clothes on, just some sort of thin nightgown that looked worn bare in spots. I looked away—I didn't want to embarrass her by seeing something I shouldn't.

Or embarrass myself, for that matter.

Mrs. Cutlin didn't beat around the bush. "What are you doing back here?"

"I came for Gayle."

"That ain't her name, kid. Don't encourage that. She'll end up in the loony bin." She opened the screen door and leaned out to spit, right next to the welcome mat. I stared at the gob of spit while she spoke.

"Suzie, you mean. Well, she didn't come back with money last time. Probably never got paid to begin with. I'm not letting that rich man take advantage of her. Now you run off, leave her be."

I fumbled for the ten-dollar bill in my jeans pocket. "He gave me this to give straight to you," I explained. Her fingers snatched the bill out of my hand as soon as it had cleared the denim. "He said it was for the whole week."

"Mr. King said that? How many snails does he got in those beds?" Mrs. Cutlin sounded suspicious. I didn't blame her. I just shrugged.

"You know how it is with rich folks. One snail, and they think they've got a thousand. She'll probably find three a day." I hazarded a peek at her face. She wasn't even looking at me; she was staring across the yard toward Mr. King's, with an expression I'd seen on my dad's face the whole week before. Disgust.

"You got that right, kid," she said. "Spoiled is what they are. More money than sense, and not a lick of neighborly kindness."

I nodded, wondering what Mrs. Cutlin thought she had done to deserve any "neighborly kindness." In the distance, a chain saw started up. "Mrs. Cutlin?" I interrupted her black thoughts about Mr. King and his money. "Is Ga—um, Suzie ready?"

Mrs. Cutlin smiled, and I realized I preferred her frowning. Her smile looked nasty, showing her cracked front teeth. "She will be." She shut the screen door in my face, and I waited for about three minutes. When Gayle came skipping out, Mrs.

Cutlin wasn't there. "Hey, Gayle," I said, soft enough no one inside would hear the name. "Why in the world are you wearing that?"

She had on a long-sleeve, brown-and-pink-plaid flannel shirt with her shorts. I thought I remembered the shirt—Isabelle had worn it practically every other day a couple of years before. Probably it had been donated to the church clothes closet, and the pastor had brought it out with the other used clothes. She hugged my waist, then ran past. "Go on," I said, "find a T-shirt, would ya!"

She just turned around, stuck her tongue out, and kept on going.

"You're going to burn up in that," I hollered at her back as she ran off ahead of me. "It's going to be over ninety degrees today!"

We spent a couple of hours poking around the garden, which pretty much had no snails at all that we could see. Well, that I could see. Gayle mostly spent her time picking thin strands of grass and sliding fallen rose petals onto them like they were beads. She ended up with a whole bunch of bracelets that looked like those Hawaiian leis—completely covered with petals. She slid them up her arms and tried to get me to wear some, too, but they were too small.

"That's not right," she said, looking at the bracelet in her hand like it had done something wrong. "Tree needs flowers, too." She raced off and made larger ones, making me put them on my arms and head—even around my neck—until I probably looked like something in a parade.

A twig cracked behind me. "You look stupid." The voice didn't scare me—I'd heard it too often. But my heartbeat sped up anyway—getting beat up all through elementary school by the kid with that voice obviously had left a mark, at least inside. "Playing baby games?"

"Hey, Jeb," I said, and stood up. "Yeah, you know me. I'm just a little baby." I crossed my arms, trying to pretend getting caught covered with flower petals wasn't as embarrassing as it felt. I was glad school was still more than a month away; maybe he'd forget this by then, wouldn't tell the whole world what I was wearing. "What are you doing over here?"

He stepped closer to me, crushing a pink flower under his foot. I thought he'd done it accidentally, but then he ground his heel into the mulch, like he was putting out a cigarette. "My mom asked me to talk to the Emperor about something."

"About what?" Was it about Gayle? I didn't want Mrs. Cutlin finding out that he hadn't asked Gayle to do gardening after all—then she'd be stuck in that house all day.

Or worse, he'd offer the money to Mrs. Cutlin, who I knew could use it, and my plans for the five hundred dollars would be so much dust. Of course, Mr. King had said Mrs. Cutlin wasn't "receptive" to discussing Gayle. Had something changed?

But that wasn't it at all. Jeb made a motion toward the fence line with one hand. "She wanted to know if he'd take that tree out."

I looked. He was pointing at Gayle's sycamore. "That one?"

"Yeah, told him the roots were tearing up the fence." He stopped, like he was thinking about something. But he was just working up a gob of spit. He let it go, and it landed on a nandina shrub. I wondered if his mom had taught him to do that, to spit right in the middle of talking to someone. "But really she just wants to put a garden in there."

I thought about that. It was pretty much the only spot on the Cutlins' property that would work for a garden—the rest was boggy. It wasn't a bad idea—and the tree was already starting to go, what with the rotten branches and all. "Sure," I said softly. I might have thought it was a good idea, but I didn't want Gayle to hear that.

"So," I said, "why don't you go ask him?"

"I just did. He said he'd talked to your dad about it. And decided not to bother." He gave me a look that said he obviously thought my dad wouldn't know any better than a kindergartner about trees. I took a step toward him, so he would remember who was bigger now.

"My dad would be the one to ask. It's his job," I said, crossing my arms over my chest so the muscles I'd worked up hauling limbs would bulge up.

He watched them, and swallowed. Then he stepped back,

shrugging. "Sure, whatever." He made a fist down at one side of his pants. "I thought I heard Suzie out here. Hey, Suzie? Where you hiding?"

I turned around. Sure enough, Gayle was gone. Had she climbed back up in her tree?

"Maybe she needed to go to the restroom," I said. "I'll tell her you were looking for her."

He laughed, and cracked his knuckles. "Don't bother. I'll see her at lunch." He said it like it was a threat.

I thought about going after him, picking a fight just to make myself feel better, but I didn't. He was right. She had to go home to his house, not me. And if I got Jeb any madder than he was, she'd suffer for it.

"Is he gone?" Gayle whispered from behind me. I whirled around. She'd been hiding under a shrub, so small and brown she'd disappeared against the mulch. So quiet I hadn't even heard her breathe.

"Yeah, he's gone." I took her hand and pulled her to her feet. "Want to go get some lunch?"

"Not at the Cutlins'," she said, her eyes darting to the house beyond the fence.

"Nah," I said. "Forget what Jeb said. I meant, in the truck. I brought an extra sandwich."

I hadn't really. I always ate two. But she didn't know that, and I could get more that night. "Ham and cheese," I teased, when she complained and said she was going to stay and make more flower crowns. "And half a Snickers bar."

She threw the flowers to the ground like so much confetti, and ran in front of me. "Race you!"

I let her win, of course. She claimed my whole Snickers bar as her prize. I didn't fuss; she was so skinny it hurt to look at her. After she'd eaten my second sandwich, she sat on the tailgate and watched while I helped Dad, clearing cut pecan limbs.

An hour or so later, Dad and I were both soaked to the skin with sweat, and I was daydreaming about a world made out of ice and Popsicles. Dad threw me a water bottle from the cooler and said I could take a break while he drove into town to pick up some more sealant. As soon as the truck roared off, Gayle came running back—she'd lit off when Dad had started in again with the chain saw, complaining that she couldn't watch her "friends" get hurt.

I sat down to rest, my back up against one of the pecans. The shade felt good, and even if it was still hot there, staying in one place was better than working in the sun. The hum of the cicadas almost made me want to take a nap.

Gayle, on the other hand, couldn't stop moving. She flitted around from tree to tree, touching them all, singing the whole time. I closed my eyes, letting the sounds wash over me.

When I opened them, she was sitting next to me, her back leaned up against my side.

"Tree?" she said.

"Little John," I reminded her, but the bees around us were buzzing the same sort of song she'd sung, a lazy, warm, sunny tune. I wasn't really mad. "What?"

"You won't let your dad cut down my tree, will you? I heard some of what Jeb said . . ." Her voice caught. "It's the only place I have."

I hesitated. I didn't want to lie to her. If the Emperor changed his mind about cutting it down, or if the Cutlins had the money to pay Dad, which I doubted, there probably wasn't anything I could do to stop him. "What's the big deal about that tree, anyway?"

"Well, duh," she said, punching me lightly in the ribs with her small fist. "It's the friendliest tree in the whole yard over there, for one thing. And for another—it's got my nest in it." I pushed back so I could see her face. She rolled her eyes at me, and for a second she looked so much like Raelynn when I'd been teasing her—full of frustration with me, but good humor, too— that tears pricked my eyes.

"Your nest?" I said, wanting to change the subject. "What's the big deal about that? You could build another one."

"No, I couldn't!" She jumped up. "That nest has all my treasures in it!"

I laughed. "Treasures? What kind of treasures does a kid your age have?" I teased her, pulling on a piece of grass stuck to her arm. "You hiding diamonds up there? Rubies and gold bricks?"

"Don't be mean," she said, her voice as frosty as my mom's when I'd let fly a cuss word right outside the church. "They're not those kinds of treasures. They're the real kind."

"Oh, the real kind?" I got up, following her as she marched off in a huff toward her yard.

"Yes," she said. "The kind you can't just . . . buy in a store."

"Oh," I said. I had wondered what she had up there, besides sticks and baling wire. "Well, don't let anyone else know you got treasures up there. They might steal 'em."

"I won't," she said. "Nobody else is allowed to see them anyway." She paused. "But you could, if you wanted to."

"Me? Climb that falling-down tree?" I laughed. "Heck, no! Not even if you had real diamonds and gold in there."

"Little John, you're being silly. That tree is perfectly good. There's nothing to be afraid of."

I just shook my head. We'd reached the fence, and I could hear Dad's truck roaring back up the road. I had to get back to work.

Then Verlie Cutlin's voice sailed out across the lawn. "Suzie? Get back in here, girl. You got dishes." I could hear the theme song for a game show drifting out the door underneath her voice. Seemed like Gayle had work to do, too.

"You gonna be okay?" I asked.

Gayle just shook her head. "I don't think I'm going to be okay anymore," she said in a broken whisper. "I don't know what I'd do, if I didn't have my tree." She grabbed hold of my legs, clinging like a clump of stickyweed. For a minute, I wasn't certain if she was talking about the sycamore—or me. But then she said, "Promise me. Promise me you won't let your dad cut down my tree."

I took a breath, then peeled her arms off me. Dad was calling for me now, too, and I had to get. "Fine," I said. "I'll do my best."

"Promise," she demanded.

I took a last look at the Cutlins' house. There was no way they would have the kind of money it took to hire my dad. They'd probably chop it down themselves, or try, anyway—if they got their lazy butts off the sofa long enough to locate an axe. There was no harm in promising this one thing, to get that sad look out of Gayle's eyes.

"I promise," I said.

Chapter 10

I'd never imagined I would look forward to working with Dad. But with Gayle around, it didn't even feel like work. Sure, I hauled limbs, burned brush, even learned to trim and seal dead limbs—a job I figured out I hated the first time I did it, since the stink of the sealant gave me a terrible headache. But the chain sawing was awesome—even if Gayle called me a meanie under her breath when I did it.

I couldn't believe it when Dad handed me the saw and told me to use it on a couple of scrubby wild persimmons that had grown up in a brushy spot. He showed me how to turn it on and explained how the safety shutoff worked. I paid close attention; I didn't want to cut my arm off or anything. But he said his saw was a good one, and that sort of thing didn't happen when you were using it right.

"Go on," he encouraged. "Just don't tell your mom I let you, okay? She'd have a fit."

"A huge one," I agreed.

We both laughed, and I was amazed to hear my own voice sound low and rich like his for a few seconds. The chain saw set my teeth to buzzing, and my arms shook with the weight and movement of it. But I did my job, and Dad clapped me on the back when I was done.

It felt good, really good. Like I was finally doing my bit to help out, help Mom and the family. The only bad part was how the whole thing made me wish like fire that Ernest was there. I could imagine how big his eyes would get, seeing me starting up the chain saw, watching me going crazy on the branches Dad pointed out. Ernest probably would have begged me to let him have a turn, like it was some video game come to life.

Gayle was the only one around, though—when I wasn't cutting trees, that is. And she made me look forward to the days at the Emperor's, even in the blistering heat. It was like I was still a kid, and we were playing all day long. Each morning, she would run over from next door as soon as she heard Dad's truck, and meet me in the garden to find the one or two snails that were there.

Both of us would pretend we didn't see Mr. King staring at us—at her—through the windows.

After the snails were gone, we'd run back across the property to help Dad. At first, he didn't want a little girl around. But when he figured out she wasn't getting underfoot, that changed.

And when he heard her singing, something else changed: He started smiling.

Once, he even tried to sing along. I couldn't believe it.

"Look at her," Dad said to me one afternoon, watching Gayle run around with her arms out like an airplane, faster and faster. Her caseworker had been out the day before, so her hair was brushed and her face was clean and shining. A flock of small birds—black-capped chickadees and sparrows, mostly—was flying right over her head, twittering almost loud enough to cover the sound of her voice. "Have you ever seen anything like that?"

I shook my head.

"She's like a ray of sunshine," he said. "Like a—like a little bird."

"Sure is," I agreed, watching the sparrows swoop lower and lower as she waved at them, like they wanted nothing more than to settle on her, make her into some sort of living tree, with arms for branches and feathers for leaves.

"Her parents?"

"She said they flew away."

"Ah," Dad said. "Poor thing." Then he shot a look toward the Cutlins' house. I knew what he was thinking. "Poor thing," he muttered again.

I guess he felt pretty sorry for her, since he started letting me take more and more time off to play with her. The Emperor had enough acreage to really roam, and the next day we did.

"Hey, Tree!" she yelled, skipping ahead, across ground studded with dead pecans and even a few scraggly prickly pears. "What's this one?" She let out a piercing stream of notes.

"A red-wing blackbird?" I guessed.

"Yep!" she yelled.

"What about this one?" I pursed my lips and let out a long, sweet whistle. It was a golden-cheeked warbler, my best birdcall.

Or it was supposed to be. Gayle almost fell down laughing at me. "What was that? A toad? A cricket being stepped on?"

"A warbler," I answered. "Never heard one?"

"Ha!" She shot over to me and blew a gorgeous birdcall— that sounded exactly like a warbler.

"Show-off," I muttered and pulled on her ponytail, not hard. I set my face into a fake scowl. "You hurt my feelings."

"I was just teasing. You're not bad, for a person," Gayle said matter-of-factly, slipping her hand into mine as we shuffled through dead leaves. "It's just that you don't make any sense when you try to speak bird."

"Make sense?" I asked, feeling the corners of my mouth twitch. "What are you going on about?"

"Well, you do say bird words. But you get 'em all jumbled up. The birds probably can't figure out what you're trying to tell 'em at all, Tree."

I was about to remind her not to call me that when she stopped stock-still and yanked hard on my hand. "Come on,

Tree! I think something's hurt, over by the fence! The birds are getting all worked up about it. Can't you hear?"

I could hear birds calling, far off, where the back corners of the property joined up. "Something's hurt? Well, you know what that means," I answered, jogging to catch up.

"What?"

I glanced back toward the work site to make sure we were far enough away. We were. "It means we gotta call an ambulance!" I put my hands around my mouth and started wailing. Gayle squealed and ran over to me, grabbing my hand. "We'll never make it in time on foot," I said. "Hop on!"

She climbed up me, hand over hand, just like she had her tree, and perched on my shoulders. "That way!" She pointed, and I followed. Weaving around up there was way too fun, and she changed the direction of her finger every second or so, to make me veer off running at a new angle. I wouldn't let her fall, of course. She was feather-light, and I had a good grip on her legs. But she screamed and laughed like she was being tickled to death up there.

My cheeks hurt from grinning, and my sides ached from laughter. For the first time in forever, I was having fun.

Finally, we got to the fence. There was something there, near the bottom of the wire. A rabbit?

"A fawn," she breathed, climbing down. "It's caught!"

It *was* caught, one of its legs tangled in a loose piece of baling wire that had been half-hidden in the weeds. I looked around, wondering how long it had been stuck. There was no momma doe nearby, as far as I could tell.

I was sure the fawn would startle and hurt itself even more, but Gayle was singing a soft, low melody. Within seconds, the fawn's eyelids were drooping . . . and so were mine. I blinked, shaking myself, and stepped lightly across the tufts of grass and weeds to help.

Gayle never stopped singing, just nodded at me to untangle the tiny thing's legs. I worked quickly, swearing under my breath at the bloodied cuts the wires had made on its delicate limbs. Some of them were deep, and they were covered in ants and small bugs. It had been here a while, suffering. "We're not going to be able to save this one," I muttered, hoping Gayle would understand. "It's been here a long time."

Gayle reached over and took my hand, settling it back on the wires. *Fine,* I thought. *I'll keep going.* It wasn't like I would hurt it any more. I worked fast, trying to ignore the dozens of finches that had been attracted by Gayle's singing and that watched me, curiously, from their perches on the wires near my shoulders.

They were sort of creeping me out, staring at me like that.

Finally, I had the wire untangled. I straightened up, wondering how the fawn had—apparently—slept through the whole thing. "That was some lullaby," I started to say, but Gayle shushed me. She laced her hands right over the torn-up places on the leg. Her song changed, to that same sort of tune she'd done when she'd gotten worried over my cut hand.

But her face was what I was paying attention to. Her features transformed, somehow. Seconds before, she had been a little girl humming a tune over a hurt fawn. Now?

She looked fierce, like a mother mockingbird dive-bombing a snake near her nest. Like she would do anything she could to help this little baby out.

I knew that feeling.

I must have been watching her face when it happened. She stopped singing, the notes dying off into the morning heat. I cleared my throat, and quicker than a wink, that fawn was up and—on its feet? How was it even standing?

I cried out, "Wait!"—dumb, like the fawn could understand me. All it did was make that little thing run faster away from us.

Gayle laughed. "It worked!"

"What?" I said, amazed that the critter had enough energy to run after being stuck in a fence for who knows how long. And with those cuts . . . "I could have sworn it was really hurt."

"Well, sure, Little John," Gayle said, taking my hand and swinging herself back up on my shoulders like a tiny monkey. "It was hurt *before*."

"Did you . . ." I paused, feeling her weight shift on my shoulders like the warm breeze was moving her. "Did you fix it?"

"Giddyap!" was all she answered, and giggled.

I laughed, too. Maybe she had healed the fawn, maybe not. All I knew for sure was that holding her on my shoulders like that made me feel a hundred feet tall. Like I was a giant and she was a fairy in some magical world that only the two of us knew about.

Like I was strong enough for anything. Like she really could fix hurts with a song.

Even if it wasn't true, I wanted to believe it for a while. The idea of it felt like a sunbeam had found its way into my usual dark thoughts and was splashing light all over the walls of my memories.

The next day at lunch, Dad shared his chips with Gayle. "Here, kid," he said, leaning across the bed of the pickup to where she was perched on one side. "You need to put some meat on those bones." His shirtsleeve pulled up when he handed her the chips, and Gayle got a look at some of the cuts on his arm, marks from the thorny vines we'd been clearing that day. I had a few, too, on my forearms where the gloves didn't cover. They stung, but they weren't a big deal. But Gayle thought Dad's were.

"You're hurt!" she cried, and grabbed Dad's arm.

"Oh, I'm fine, honey," he said. "This ain't nothing."

"Want me to make it better?" she asked, her eyes as still and serious as I'd ever seen.

Dad didn't answer for a second. I looked over. He was staring at the ham sandwich on his lap. His Adam's apple was bobbing up and down, though, like he was swallowing over and over. Then I understood.

Raelynn had asked that, every time Dad had come home from work with even a tiny scratch or cut. She'd insisted on kissing every cut better.

"I'd . . . I'd better go see to that redbud tree now," Dad said, instead of answering. He got up and walked behind the truck, disappearing to check on some imaginary problem. I was pretty sure Mr. King didn't have any redbud trees.

"Did I hurt his feelings?" Gayle asked me. "What did I say?"

"Nothing," I said, moving to sit on the lowered tailgate of the truck where Dad had been. "It's just you reminded him of Raelynn. She used to do that. Kiss it and make it better."

"I wasn't going to kiss it," Gayle said after a few seconds. "I was going to sing it better."

"Same thing, sort of," I said, rubbing at the place where I'd cut my hand on the Cutlins' screen door. The night before, away from Gayle, I had pretty much convinced myself I'd made it all up—my arm, the fawn. But maybe she could heal after all. Her song had made Dad happy, hadn't it? Or close to it. And he hadn't smiled in ten months.

After a few moments, I heard Dad walking back.

But it wasn't Dad. It was Mr. King. Then, in a rush of

sound—the swish of bare feet on grass—I knew Gayle had run off. What was it about Mr. King that made her so shy?

"Hello, sir," I said, hopping down off the truck. "Can I help you?"

"I hope so," he said. "It's been a week."

"Not quite," I said, then remembered myself, "sir. Tomorrow's a week."

"Have you asked her to sing for me yet?"

"Well," I said.

His brows drew down, and I had the feeling he was about to say something I would regret.

"But I'm going to today," I rushed out. "And she likes me, and my dad. She'll get used to the idea. Then we can do it—"

"Tomorrow," he said, and his voice was like bark peeling off a birch tree.

"Yes, sir," I said, but he was already walking away.

Chapter 11

The next morning, I was nervous. I didn't know why. I think because I had told Gayle to meet me in the garden, and I had a feeling it was going to be harder to convince her to sing for Mr. King than I'd hoped. Maybe it was because Mrs. Cutlin had phoned the house the night before, asking how much it would cost to get her sycamore taken out. Why I would worry about that, though, I didn't know. It wasn't going to happen. Dad had quoted her his price—a good price, at that—and she had laughed at him, then offered an amount so stupidly low, he laughed right back.

Maybe I was nervous because Dad had told me we had a lot of work to do that day, so I couldn't play with Gayle. But I told him I had to at least meet her, and check on the snails.

But when I got to the garden, she wasn't there. The only trace of Mr. King was the twitching of a curtain. The only other sign of life was the buzz of Dad's chain saw, the pitch rising up and down as he cut.

Then a crow flew high overhead, cawing. It sounded excited, like it had found something to eat. Or something to take back to its nest. For some reason, the noise made me jumpy.

I was just about to leave when Gayle came running up. "Good morning," she yelled. "Look what I made you!" She motioned for me to lean down, and put at least a half dozen flower necklaces over my head.

"Wow, Gayle," I said. "That's a lot of flowers. What did you do, raid Mr. King's garden in the night?"

"No. The birds brought me 'em," she answered. I didn't even want to know what that meant, so I went on.

"Listen, Gayle, I gotta go help my dad today. So why don't you hold on to these necklaces for me—"

I started to take them off, but she stopped me. "Oh no! I've got enough for your dad, too!" She held up another big wreath that she'd strung with petals and silver sage leaves. It was beautiful, like the engravings of leaves and flowers on the margins of one of my bird books. "Where is he?" She tilted her head in one direction, then the other, listening as the chain saw roared back to life in the distance. "Oh. Cutting more of those poor trees. I wish he'd stop." She set the wreath back down. "We'd better get the snails quick today, Little John. Your dad's flowers might not last."

Five minutes later, we'd picked three snails out of the rose garden—ignoring the swaying curtains in the house. Gayle had been humming under her breath the whole time. It was like working next to a mockingbird—there was everything from snatches of radio songs to commercial jingles to frog calls in her made-up melodies.

"Hey, Little John," Gayle said, tapping me on my arm with an empty snail shell.

"Just a second," I said, trying to work a nasty splinter out of my thumb.

"But your dad's calling." She was right. I hadn't heard him at first, but now I did. And he sounded angry.

I didn't blame him. He'd warned me he really needed me today. There was too much work for one man to do. I had to pull my weight.

"Let's go," she said, hanging the wreath back on her arm.

I took a deep breath. "Just give it to him, and then you'll leave?"

"Sure," she promised, but her voice was full of mischief. Dad wasn't going to like this.

"Little John!" I heard again, the voice far away, and then a truck horn honking three times.

"Better hurry," Gayle said.

"I'm gonna run," I warned her. "Hop on my back?" I held my hands out as stirrups.

"Pony ride!" she shouted, and scrambled up. If anything, she felt lighter than the day before. Weren't the Cutlins feeding her?

"Go!" she yelled, digging her fingers into my shoulders. I galloped with a stride designed to throw off little cowgirls—but she stayed on, hooting and singing, all the way to the far side of the property.

Dad was leaning on the truck with a bottle of water in one hand. "What's she here for?" he said, not looking at Gayle or me. "I told you she couldn't be out here today." His face was streaked with sweat, even though he'd been working for less than half an hour, and he was rubbing at a spot on his back like he'd pulled something. There was an impressive stack of cut logs next to the truck, though. I whistled. "Nice job, Dad." Gayle climbed off my back. "I can get these. I'll load 'em up." I grabbed the first pecan log—heavy, not rotten wood at all—and rolled it across the truck bed. "Gayle, you stay out of the way," I warned.

But Gayle wasn't there. She was standing next to my dad, who already had a wreath on his neck, and her hand was out. What else was she giving him? A rosebud, it looked like. "This is for you," she said. "Because you're sad."

"Sad?" Dad reared back, like he'd been stung. "Sad, huh. You get on away from here, now. It's not safe." He shot me a look, and I hurried to gather a few more logs. "Fool boy, bringing the little girl out on a work site," he muttered. "Go on, now. Get." Gayle just set the rosebud down on top of the biggest log, patting the cut piece like it was a dead pet or something. Eventually, she wandered off, picking dandelions and primroses and weaving the stems together.

She had walked off a little ways when Dad finally said something, under his breath. "What's with her?"

"Huh?"

His lips quirked. "With the singing and the flowers. You been around her a lot. Is she crazy, like they say?" For a minute, we both got quiet, thinking about someone else we knew who was sort of nuts, but with ribbons instead of flowers. Mom had been . . . a little off, that morning.

I shook my head. "I don't think so. Living with Mrs. Cutlin would make anybody nuts, though." We both stopped loading wood for a second and considered Gayle, who had pulled some small branches and was stripping them and forming them into some kind of a circle. "I think she's just lonely."

"Her parents died how again?" Dad asked, hefting another three logs into the truck bed. I glanced down at my own log and reached for another. If he could do three at a time, I could do two.

I wasn't going to tell him about what Gayle had said—that her parents were going to come back. I settled for "dunno" and reached for one more log, trying not to grunt with the effort. We kept on that way for a while, him bending and lifting more and more logs at a time and me trying to match him. We were both sweating so hard by then, it looked like we'd been swimming with all our clothes on.

We got to the end of the pile, to the biggest ones—stumps, more than logs. There was no way I was going to be able to pick one of those up.

"Think we can do it together?" Dad pulled one of his work gloves off and wiped his forehead with the back of his hand. "On three?"

My stomach flipped at the thought of trying to lift the mammoth log. "Maybe," I said after a second. "Shouldn't we cut it up first?"

"Nah," Dad said, and put his glove back on. "This one's for the furniture guy. He'll make an end table out of it, or something. Nice," he said, slipping his hand over the cut end. It was beautiful wood, with a pattern I could see even through the cuts from the saw. "Wood like this, it's worth something." He stroked it again, but it didn't look like he was thinking of how much money it was worth. It looked like he was admiring it.

"One . . . ?" Dad started, settling his hands on one side of the stump. I knelt on the other side. "That's right, son, bend at the knees. Two?"

I nodded, hearing my heart pound over the sound of Gayle's distant singing. "Three!" Dad yelled, and we both lifted.

At first, I thought the stump was going to tip over onto me— the side Dad held was going up too fast, and my arms weren't strong enough to catch it. But then he shifted his hand and took some of the weight off my side, and I was able to straighten my knees a little bit. I heard Dad ask something—it sounded like "Got it?"—but I couldn't answer. The muscles in my chest felt wrong, like something inside was stretching, tearing. I was holding my breath, counting the small, shuffling steps I took to the truck bed. "Now!" I heard Dad shout, and we lifted the log a bit higher.

Ouch! Something inside me definitely popped, and I felt a sharp, hot pain, like boiling water poured inside my chest, but I held on to my end of the log. Finally, Dad nodded, and we dropped it, letting it roll into the truck bed.

My ears were ringing, and small bright lights bobbed around in front of my eyes when I let go. I leaned against the open tailgate, sucking in breath after breath, rubbing my chest.

"You . . . okay?" Dad breathed from the other side of the bumper. I tried to focus on him. He was in the same position as I was, leaned over, huffing and puffing, but he took the steps over and clapped me on the arm. "Great job, son," he said. "That was man's work. I'm awful glad I had you here." He paused. "Proud of ya."

I swallowed. It was the first time I could ever remember him saying that. Proud of me. My chest stopped hurting for a few seconds, and I smiled.

"Thanks, Dad," I said. He nodded, and looked away, toward

Gayle. We both did, just stared at her, listening to her sing. She'd found something on the ground and was singing to it.

"She's not pretty," he said at last. I felt the corners of my mouth turn down, until he finished. "But it doesn't matter, not with that singing of hers. It's . . . beautiful, isn't it?" I nodded and closed my eyes, listening to it. With every note, it seemed like my chest hurt less.

Wait. It *did* hurt less. I knew I'd pulled something; I'd felt it go. But now . . . I took a deep breath. Nothing. I opened my eyes, wondering if Dad had noticed anything. He was leaning back, eyes shut. Gayle was still singing—and what was that in her hand? Something alive, it looked like, but I couldn't tell.

"Go on and play with her," Dad said. "I'll drive the truck back up to the house and ask Mr. King if this is enough wood for his furniture guy."

"Okay," I said. By the time Dad had gotten into the cab of the truck, I'd reached Gayle's side and found out what she'd been up to.

"A bunny, Gayle? Seriously?" I leaned down. Gayle stopped singing.

"A baby," she said. "Almost dead. Worse than the fawn. I sang it better." I reached down and stroked the tiny thing. It trembled, warm and soft under my hand.

"It was hurt?" I asked.

"Almost dead," she repeated. "I never sung anything back

that was so bad off. It means I'm growing up."

"What's that, then? You think you're big now?" I stood up and pretend-shouted down to her. "I can't hear you so far down there. You know, you look like an ant from this high up."

"Stop making fun, Little John," she groused. "You know I can heal things. You saw it."

"I saw . . . something," I admitted. My heart was beating faster, remembering the fawn. "I'm not sure."

She rolled her eyes at me. "You're just chicken," she said. "Chicken they'll think you're as crazy as they think I am."

"Well, that makes sense," I said slowly. "With you being a nightingale and all. It's only right I should be a chicken." I set off clucking and flapping my arms, making rooster sounds and hen squawks. Finally, when I laid an imaginary egg right on top of Gayle's head, she got up, laughing.

"It's not funny, you know," she said. "This bunny's the only one left." She pulled my hand and led me around the tree. There, a few feet away, was a mound of grass, with scraps of fur to one side. From what I could see, there had been at least three bunnies that hadn't made it. "I think a dog got 'em," she said. "Jeb said there's a black dog around here."

"I've seen it," I said. I had, the first day we'd come out here to work. It had slunk around the truck, looking for scraps, probably, until Dad had thrown some rocks at it and chased it off. "It's a stray."

"He said he was gonna get it to bite me." Gayle pushed the grass to one side and settled the lone bunny back in the low place that had been dug out by its mother. "I don't like Jeb."

"Is that why you built that nest?" I asked, watching as Gayle picked up her flower wreaths and settled them around her neck. She had made three, and the pink primroses matched the check on her shirt.

"No," she said, rolling her eyes at me again and sighing. "I built the nest so my parents could find me, like they said to if I ever got lost from 'em. And for my treasures." She held out her hand. "I'll show you."

I just shook my head. "I'm not climbing that tree, and you're not either. It has a bad limb, you know. Dad and I are supposed to trim it this week."

"You won't hurt it, though?" Gayle said, eyes wide. "You won't hurt my nest?"

"Of course not," I said, hoping I wasn't lying. For all I knew, the bad limb was the very one she'd built her nest on. But I didn't say that.

"Okay," she said slowly. "You promise?"

"Another promise? I already promised not to let Dad cut the tree down, didn't I?"

"But the nest, Little John," she insisted. "You won't hurt it either. Right?"

I shook my head. When I was her age, I guess I wanted promises, too. Heck, I'd spit-sworn with Ernest that we'd be friends forever. And look what had happened there, what I'd done.

I'd learned better than to make promises. But I could probably keep this one. I mean, I wouldn't be the one cutting the limb, right? Dad did that part. He just wanted to teach me how to seal the cut. And I had an idea anyway—a way to get that five hundred dollars. "Sure," I said. "If you'll do something for me."

"What?"

"Well, I want you to sing," I began.

Gayle laughed. "Little John, I been singing all day!" She jumped up and grabbed hold of one of my legs. Using my hips and arms like branches, she climbed until she was all the way up on my shoulders.

"I know," I said. "I meant I wanted you to sing for the Emperor."

She stopped laughing, and swiveled around, so she could see my face. "For . . . for Mr. King?" Her voice trembled when she said his name. "Why him?"

I shrugged, trying not to meet her eyes. "He likes your singing. It's not a big deal, is it? He has a room in his house. You'd like it. There's lots of music stuff in there."

"I don't know," she said, slowly. "I don't sing inside very much. It sounds better outside."

"Well, it wouldn't hurt to sing one song for him, would it

now?" I didn't mention anything about the recording. It didn't matter, did it? Maybe once Mr. King recorded it, he'd leave her alone. He could just listen to the recording, right?

"You want me to do it?" she asked, and her voice was softer now. She had turned back around and was clinging to my neck like a burr. Tight, like she thought I might run off and leave her at any second. "Would you be there, too?"

"Of course," I said, remembering the look in the Emperor's eyes when he'd threatened me and my father. "I'll stay the whole time."

"Okay," she said softly, and tucked her face against my hair. I could feel her hot breath push against my neck.

"Fine," I said. "How about tomorrow?"

She didn't answer. I changed the subject. "Aren't you scared up there, Gayle?" I said. "I used to try to give shoulder rides to"—I almost said Raelynn, but changed it—"to my friend's sister, Isabelle, and she always screamed like I was gonna drop her. Sometimes I did drop her, you know. Not on purpose."

Gayle laughed once against my hair. "Silly," she said, "you'd never let me fall." Then she dug her heels into my sides, just hard enough to startle me, and yelled, "Giddyap!"

I laughed and reared back like a stallion, then started racing around the clearing, swerving past the pecan trees. I held on to her thin legs, though, making sure I didn't drop her.

I laughed with her, but inside her words pounded against

my racing heart. The same heart that was somersaulting at the thought of five hundred dollars, five hundred dollars for me and Mom and Dad. Gayle believed in me. "You'd never let me fall," she'd said.

I prayed it was true.

But I found out the next day it wasn't true at all.

Chapter 12

On the way to Mr. King's the next morning, Dad asked me if Gayle was going to be there.

"I think so," I said. "If that's all right? I mean, she won't be in the way or anything?" I didn't think Dad had minded her running around the day before, especially not after she had put those flower wreaths on his head. He'd laughed harder than I'd heard in years when she'd whispered in his ear, "You're the *real* Emperor."

While they were eating a snack, I'd sneaked back over to the house—I told Dad it was to go to the bathroom, but really it was to tell the Emperor I'd convinced Gayle to sing the next day.

"Can I have the money now?" I'd asked him. But he shook his head.

"A deal's a deal, son," he'd said. "You'll get the money after she sings, not before."

I worried that he'd try to cheat me, but there was nothing I could do. I shook the thought away to listen to my dad.

"She's a strange little thing," Dad said, looking in the rear-view mirror at the car that was honking behind us. We were going pretty slow, but it was just because his truck was so old and broken down. Dad took his foot off the accelerator and pushed the brakes a few times, smiling at the mirror when the car honked again.

"Gayle?" I asked, hoping it wasn't one of the kids from school in the car. I scooched down in my seat a little as the car finally passed us. "Yeah, she is. But I told her she could come back over today. I hope that was okay, sir."

"Sure, son," he said, and he laid a hand on my arm. "I think that's a good idea."

"You do?"

"I do. I saw those marks on her arms the other day." He spat out his open window and shook his head. "Verlie Cutlin shouldn't be allowed to foster."

"Marks on her arms?" I asked, remembering the fingerprints from the week before. I hadn't seen any marks yesterday, though—she'd mostly been wearing long sleeves. *That* was why she'd had her shirt all buttoned up.

"How bad were they?" I asked, not wanting to hear. "Should we tell someone?"

"Well," Dad said, "it's hard to prove anything when you

don't see it happen. But if it gets much worse . . . we'll see. Not till this job's done, though. We can't mess with all that until we have some money."

"If she's really hurt, Dad, we have to say something now!" My voice was too loud, and I tried to talk calmly. "That's more important than money, isn't it?"

"More important than a roof over your head? Than clothes on your momma's back?"

I had to work not to roll my eyes. He was one to talk. I couldn't remember the last time Mom had money enough for clothes that Dad hadn't gone and drunk it away before she had a chance to drive into Brownwood and spend it.

I must've made some sound, because Dad shot me a look. "You keep your trap shut. The little girl will be all right. She can stay over at Mr. King's with us."

I stared out the window, disgusted with him, until it dawned on me: I wasn't any better. I had convinced Gayle to do something she didn't really want to, for money. Even if it was just singing.

I shut my eyes against the warm wind that blew through my open window, and wished I wasn't like my father—strong on the outside, weak on the inside.

Mr. King was waiting for us on his front porch. He was dressed even fancier than the day before, like he was going to the opera or something.

Or hosting his own little opera.

He nodded at my dad and asked if I could help out in his garden again that day. "Sure," Dad said slowly, looking at me with a question in his eyes. I shook my head and—my back turned to Mr. King—rolled my eyes. "I can handle snails, Dad. I'll get it done in less than an hour so we can trim that sycamore branch."

"Fine," Dad said, obviously uncomfortable with leaving me there. "I'll call when I need you."

I grabbed my water bottle from the truck and ran around back. I could already hear Gayle singing in her nest, so I knew right where to go to get her. "Get down from there," I yelled. "I told you that tree has a bad branch." A hundred birds took flight when they heard my voice, though, and for a second, I couldn't even see Gayle for all the fluttering wings. The birds twittered angrily, and at least two of them pooped on my shirt as they left. I wiped it off, and frowned up at the nest. I couldn't even see Gayle's head—she had to be hunkered down really low. Was she hiding from someone? "Gayle?"

"Oh, it's you," she called back, and scrambled down, carrying something in her hand. "I got something for you," she said. She popped her head over the top of the wooden fence—how had she climbed it that fast? *I swear,* I thought, *the girl is at least half-bird herself. Or squirrel*—and shook her closed fist at me. "Well, come on," she said, "it's for you."

"What is it?" I asked, taking her wrist to help her hop

off the fence. When she was on Mr. King's side, she let out a giant breath, like she'd gotten away from something. *Jeb?* I wondered. She was in a long-sleeve shirt again—the same one as yesterday and the day before. It was dirty as all get out, and her hair had more sticks in it than a real bird's nest. "Hang on," I said, and started picking at the twigs, throwing them down.

"Stop it," she said. "That don't matter. This does."

She opened her fist. In the palm of her hand was a rock. It wasn't just a rock, though, it was quartz, and someone had shined it up until it sparkled like diamonds in the sunlight. "Oh, that's pretty," I said, taking it. "Are you sure you want to give it to me? I don't have anything for you."

"You can bring me something tomorrow," she said. "And when you get done being scared of climbing trees, you can see my nest. It's got all sorts of good stuff in it. You'd like it. I'll let you pick three more things, maybe." She smiled like a cat. "But you gotta climb up."

"I'm not climbing that tree," I said, my heart pounding at the very thought. "And I'm sure as heck not gonna go out on a branch that might be rotten." My voice must have sounded sharper than I intended, because Gayle's lip quivered.

"But I like this rock an awful lot," I said. "Thank you."

She didn't say *you're welcome*, just put her hand in mine and walked with me toward the Emperor's house.

"I still don't like him," she said, as we got close enough to see the man's face peeking through the curtains at the back window.

"I know," I said. I didn't say what else I was thinking—*me neither*. "But he's all alone. And he wants to hear you sing." I shrugged. "I can understand it. Your voice is...something else."

"For you." Gayle hugged my waist and followed me up the porch steps to the back door.

The door opened as we got there, and the Emperor stepped out. "Welcome, dear girl," he said to Gayle. He was holding a handful of peppermint candy canes out to her like birdseed to a pigeon. He looked kind of like a creepy kidnapper, and I had a thought about grabbing Gayle and turning her around.

But she surprised me. She smiled and shook her head. "It's hard to sing my best with food in my mouth. Momma always said to eat afters."

"Oh." Mr. King looked at me, obviously confused. He straightened up. "Well, I'll save it for you for...afters."

It was strange, entering the house from the back. The hallway we walked into couldn't have been more different from the front—instead of wood paneling and fancy china plates, there were oil paintings of sunflowers and sunsets. I blinked and stepped closer to one of the paintings. The sunflowers in it had faces. Smiling sunflowers? It reminded me of my aunt Linda's paintings, the hobby she'd taken up after her husband—Mom's brother, her only family left alive by then—had died. For six years, until Aunt Linda followed him, everyone in the family had received an original masterpiece, usually of ladybugs with too many spots or happy bumblebees with eyes bigger than their wings. I had three of them in my room.

Gayle giggled. "I like them," she whispered.

Mr. King must have heard, since he stopped and cleared his throat. "Thank you. My wife, Inga. She loved to paint." He paused again. "She was a singer, too. I would listen to her for hours . . ."

I didn't say anything. Neither did Gayle. We just looked at each other, then back at Mr. King. I didn't know if it was the hallway, or his expression, but somehow, he didn't seem so threatening anymore. He seemed small, like he'd shrunk over-night. Empty. His wife had died, I guess. I felt kind of sorry for him.

I guess Gayle did, too. "Listen," she said, and—still hold-ing mine—she took his hand and began to sing. Outside, the sound had traveled over the grass and through the soft morning air. In the cool hallway, it was almost overwhelmingly beautiful. Somehow, in her song, I could hear a story.

A bird, flying alone, far from home, wings beating until the bird began to falter and fall to the ground below. The wind whistled through its wings, through splayed, worn-out feathers. The bird sighed into the cold air one last time, its eyes almost closing . . . and then, something appeared. Glimmered, there, at the edge of the horizon. A tree? An aspen, with shining leaves that turned and caught the fading light, then called in a voice like a mermaid's, "Come here, come home." Its branches, streaming leaves of silver in the air, waved and beckoned, guiding the bird home.

The song stopped. I opened my eyes. The Emperor was standing there, his hand in hers, his body shaking. His eyes were shut, but tears were streaming down his face, past his nose and his . . . smile?

"Thank you, child," he said, and Gayle smiled up at him, the dirt on her face less obvious in this light. She could have been his granddaughter, from the way they were looking at each other.

"Do you feel better?" she asked. "Can we go outside now?" She smiled at me. "Tree's dad is calling."

"Tree?" Mr. King looked confused.

"Little John," she corrected herself. I heard Dad then, too, calling my name. Wondering where I was, it sounded like, and none too happy.

"Yes, I do feel better," he said, "But won't you sing for me one more time?" He started to pull her into the hallway, toward his music room. I followed a few steps behind.

Gayle looked toward me, worry creasing her face. "But we have to go," she said, whimpered.

"One more song, dear," he said, "and then candy, remember?"

Gayle brightened at that. "Can I have more than one?" she asked.

"John!" I heard Dad's voice, too loud, in the backyard.

"I gotta go," I said, wondering what to do.

"We'll be fine, won't we?" Mr. King asked Gayle. "Go on and help your dad. We're just going to sing and then eat some candy." He nodded at me, impatient for me to go. "I'll pay you later."

"Gayle?" I said. Had she picked up on that—the paying part? But she hadn't. She was staring at the plates on the wall in the dark hallway ahead of us.

"Birds," she said softly. She walked over to one and touched the metal prongs of the plate hangers that held them, claw-like, fastened to the wall. "They're all birds."

"Yes," said Mr. King. But he wasn't looking at the plates; he was staring at her. Light glinted in his eyes. They looked more than ever like a crow's—wanting to collect the shiny thing it saw, steal it, and take it back to its nest.

His voice was soft, mesmerizing. "I love birds, don't you? I have a special sort of aviary, did you know that?" And with that, before I could protest again, he led her into the recording room and shut the door.

"John!" My dad's voice carried all the way into the front hallway, and I ran for the door. If I didn't show my face, I was going to be in a lot more danger than Gayle might be.

I'd apologize to her later.

"I'll be back in an hour," I promised the closed door, and raced out into the hot cicada buzz of late morning.

Chapter 13

I'd never worked so hard or so fast in my life. Dad had yelled for a while, then given me an extra job to do before lunch, my punishment for "running off to play." He made me promise to apologize to Mr. King for not doing the gardening like he'd asked—I didn't explain there hadn't ever been any gardening to do in the first place; that would raise too many questions. All I could think about the whole time I was splitting wood was Gayle. My axe would rise, and I would remember the look in her eyes when he took her hand—and the axe would fall, and the sound was that of the recording room door slamming shut. Before I knew it, I was out of logs to split.

"Where's the girl?"

I jumped. Dad had walked up behind me so quietly, I hadn't heard a thing. "Here," he said, and handed me my water bottle, full again with icy water from the big cooler he kept in the back of the truck.

"Thanks."

"The girl?" he asked again.

"Oh, I think she went around back of the Emperor's house," I said. "Looking for snails? I saw her a while ago," I lied. "Maybe I oughta go check on her."

Dad just spat into the grass. "Don't let me hear you say that, son. Ever." His voice was like a coiled rattlesnake.

"What, sir?" I blinked. His brows had lowered like I'd done something terrible. Did he know I'd lied? I flushed hot, then cold.

"Don't you ever let me hear you call him Emperor," Dad said, each word slow and precise. "He's nothing but a man. A man who made money off honest folk's work. And I've heard worse, too. He's spoiled, used to getting his way. Remember one thing—just because a man's rich don't mean he's good. You call him Mr. King, and nothing else. And don't trust him."

"Yes, sir," I said, taking another swig of water, pouring some on my overheated neck. With every word Dad said, I felt worse about leaving Gayle. "Can I go check on her now?" I asked. I was starting to get worried. She hadn't come out of the house, not out here anyway. That was an awful long time to record one song. If anything happened to her . . . it would be my fault. I had promised her I'd be there.

A flock of starlings shot past overhead, screeching like they were being chased by something fearsome. They were flying as fast as they could, straight away from Mr. King's house.

Something was wrong. "I gotta go!" I burst out and took off running.

I was at the house in less than a minute.

I didn't bother knocking. I grabbed the door handle, but it wouldn't turn.

Locked. It hadn't been locked before. Then I did knock, loud, on the wood. I looked for a bell, but there wasn't one. Just a large brass knocker hanging in the middle of the door, a lion with a loop of metal in his teeth. His eyes glared down at me. I lifted the knocker but dropped it back down when I heard something—a laugh? a cry? a cough?—coming from inside.

The back door.

I ran. My feet crushed the blue flowers where they fell, rose brambles scraped my arms as I ignored the pathway—it was too far from the rear of the house—and cut through the garden.

I ran through the door, which was still unlocked. *That was good, right?* I thought. Nothing too terrible could happen inside an unlocked house.

I knew I was just trying to make myself feel better. It wasn't working. The back hallway was empty, and I raced for the recording room, hoping Gayle was all right.

I never should have left her, I thought. *I should have listened to her.*

I had just reached the door to the recording room when a shaft of light fell across the carpet at my side.

"John? What are you doing?" It was Mr. King, standing in the doorway to what looked like a kitchen. I could see a stove behind him, a large stainless steel one, with more knobs and handles than I'd ever seen on an appliance. A stove, and behind it a sink . . . and Gayle standing in front of the sink, her back to me. She was looking out the window. I couldn't see her face, couldn't tell if she was upset.

"Gayle," I said, shouldering past Mr. King. "Gayle? It's time to go."

She turned to me. She didn't look upset—or at least she hadn't been crying—but her eyes reminded me of my mother's. Hollow, and haunted.

Gayle paused, like she was going to say something. She even opened her mouth and worked her jaw like she was trying to talk. But no sounds came out.

Like whatever she had to tell me, she couldn't bear to say yet.

She let out a rattling breath and pushed past me without looking at my face. Her hand was closed around what looked like a candy cane, one that had been licked until the sticky red candy had oozed over her fingers.

Her fingers were white, like she'd been holding the candy too tightly, for too long.

"Good-bye, dear," Mr. King said to her. His smile was satisfied. "You can come over anytime. I'd love to record your voice again. And you're welcome to listen to the recording a few more times as well—it will help you learn to hear the flaws, and correct them." He shook his head. "I wish I had the expertise to truly train your voice. Maybe if I hired an instructor to come to my house and help you, they could—" he broke off. "Never mind that."

He reached out to touch her hair as she passed, but Gayle shrank back.

She practically ran out of the room, leaving me to face Mr. King on my own. Which was just what I wanted.

I took a ragged breath. "What did you do to her?" My voice seemed to get lower with each word, and I straightened up, stepping closer until I towered over him. He had a bald spot on the top of his head, a shiny round one the size of a chicken's egg. I wanted to smash it, to pound my fists into it until he told me what had made Gayle run away like that.

"What are you talking about?" he asked, his smile as slick as oil on pond water. "I recorded Gayle's voice. She has the most amazing voice, you know." His eyes grew unfocused. And then, unconsciously, he licked his lips. "So artless, so trusting."

Trusting? I wondered what he was talking about. "What did you do?" I yelled into his face.

No smile now. "Exactly what I intended. I added her voice to my collection," he said, his brows low. "Thank you for bringing her over. Now get out of my house." He glanced down at my work clothes, and I was suddenly aware of the wide sweat stains from the morning's work and the small rips in my shirt I'd earned cutting his trees. "Don't worry. You'll get your money."

Like money was all I cared about. Like he could pay me for the look in Gayle's eyes.

I was afraid. Not afraid of him, although the memory of his threat rang in my mind. No, I was afraid I might punch him if I stayed that close. So I turned on my heel and left the kitchen, following the way I thought Gayle would have taken.

The back door was slightly open, and I ran through it, not bothering to shut it myself. I ran toward the Cutlins' property, stopping at the fence.

"Gayle?" I called. There were no birds in the sycamore, no singing coming from the nest. But I knew she was there.

"Gayle?" I said softer. "Are you all right?"

The nest trembled a little, and I heard a soft hiccup of a sob.

In the distance, a crow cawed, ugly and short. She didn't answer, didn't speak.

"What happened?" I asked, feeling something growing inside me, something red and twisted, smoking like a bonfire fed too much fuel, too fast. "What happened in there?"

Another sob was all I heard, and then an exhalation, thready and slow, like Gayle had decided breathing was too hard, and she was giving it up.

I wanted to climb the tree, to crawl into the nest with her. I put my hand on the fence. I would climb over. I would climb the tree, talk to her. I didn't have to be afraid of a stupid tree.

But I couldn't make myself move—the thought of going up there made me break out in a cold sweat.

"Gayle, come down," I panted. "Talk to me."

I heard my dad's voice far behind me, calling my name. "Little John! Get back here!"

I hated myself. But I had too much hate building up inside to spend it all on me. "I'm coming," I promised. But I wasn't answering my dad. I was talking to Mr. King.

I turned and walked—no, stalked—back to Mr. King's house.

He and I were going to have words. I knew it wasn't smart; in fact, it was plain stupid.

But staring up at Gayle's nest, I'd felt scared and sick, the way I'd felt ten months before, watching my little sister twist like a fast-falling leaf, plummet toward the ground in front of me, while I couldn't help her—couldn't reach her. I had been too small, too weak.

I wasn't small and weak now. I was strong and big. I hadn't protected Raelynn. And now, when I'd decided to watch out for Gayle, I'd let her down, too.

Maybe I couldn't chop down every tree in the world to keep all the little girls safe. But I could make sure that man in the fancy house never got near one again.

Chapter 14

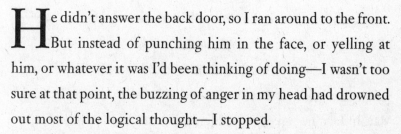

He didn't answer the back door, so I ran around to the front. But instead of punching him in the face, or yelling at him, or whatever it was I'd been thinking of doing—I wasn't too sure at that point, the buzzing of anger in my head had drowned out most of the logical thought—I stopped.

My dad was standing there with him, the two of them leaning over the front railing and talking like they were old friends. I couldn't believe it—I didn't believe it. Dad hated Mr. King.

"Why are you talking to him?" I blurted out. "You don't know what he's done."

Both of the men looked down the railing at me, but only Dad spoke. "Boy, you better watch that mouth of yours," he said. "Show some respect." His eyes said more than that—they were full of anger, and caution, and—fear?

My dad was afraid, afraid of Mr. King.

"Respect?" I almost yelled the word. "Do you know what kind of man this is?"

Dad practically sprang from the porch, reaching me in three long steps. He grabbed my arm and twisted it so hard I cried out. "Not another word," he hissed between clenched teeth. "What's got into you?"

I hissed back. "He did something to Gayle." Dad's fingers let go the smallest bit, and I wrenched away.

"What's this?" Dad said, turning to Mr. King, but not meeting his eyes. "Was that little girl over to your house?" His voice shook a little, but I couldn't tell if it was anger or something else.

"Yes." Mr. King blinked at us, like the sun was too bright all of a sudden. "Your son brought her over like we agreed yesterday. In fact, he ran off so suddenly, I wasn't able to pay him."

"Pay him?" my dad growled. His gaze was back on me, full of anger and confusion. "Pay him for what?"

Mr. King stepped off the porch, too, his shiny black shoes squeaking against the waxed wood of the steps. He pulled out his wallet as he walked and unfolded a stack of bills from inside. "Here you are, boy," he said, holding out more money than I'd ever seen, shaking it at me to take it. "Five hundred dollars, like we promised."

"Five hundred dollars?" Dad asked. "What did you do, son?" His eyes were on me, and I felt the hot burn of shame wash

across my face. I had to explain it wasn't me who had done anything—but I knew better. I had left Gayle here, with this man
with crow's eyes.

"Ask him," I said. "Ask him what he did."

Mr. King just shook his head at me and my dad. "I wish
I knew what you were talking about. You brought Gayle here
to be recorded, in exchange for five hundred dollars. Like we
agreed."

"Why would you give him five hundred dollars for that?"
My dad was still growling, but not at me. Maybe he'd figured
out what I was too late in realizing—that a man like Mr. King
didn't give up that much money for nothing. "Recording what?"

"Her voice," he said. "Her singing. And I'm not sure I like
your tone."

"That's a lot of money, is all," Dad said. "Too much."

"Well, to tell the truth," Mr. King answered, "I thought you
could use the money. I know it's been hard for your family since
the funeral."

"Oh," Dad said at last. "I see." He shot me a look that promised a beating when we got home.

"You saw? You don't see anything!" I sputtered, but Dad's
fingers got tight on my arm again, and I stopped.

"Take the money, son," he said, as Mr. King shook the bills
at my face again.

"No," I said, the word slicing through my throat.

"Take it," Dad repeated, and shoved me toward Mr. King. The bills fluttered in the breeze that blew past our faces, warm and smelling of roses and crushed earth. The numbers at their corners teased me, all those twenties, even fifties. I'd never held a fifty-dollar bill, only ever seen one in the offering plate at church.

I wanted it, bad. But I knew I shouldn't touch it.

For a second, I considered it. Maybe it didn't matter. It wasn't like I was going to spend it on myself. Taking the money would help Mom at least. Rent was due Friday, and maybe we'd have enough left over for her to buy a dress.

I could still apologize to Gayle, find some way to make it up to her. Maybe I'd buy her something.

I reached and took the money out of his hand, careful not to touch the man's skin. Wondering if you could catch evil like the flu.

And then, as I was stepping back, the Emperor made his final mistake. He let the victory creep into his dark brown eyes, the corners of his mouth twitching upward in relief.

He'd done it. He'd bought me, and he knew it.

"You're a bad man," I said. "And I don't want nothing of yours." I took the clump of bills and flung them at his face, wishing they were harder, sharper, wishing I could cut him up the way I was cut up inside after hearing Gayle cry. But the bills just fluttered around his surprised face, like molting feathers, falling to the ground below.

"Little John!" Dad shouted. I didn't listen. I turned and ran, ran back toward the road.

Away from the sycamore tree, and the nest, and the little girl I'd given up for money. Away from Mr. King, the man who had done something to make her shrink back from him, like she was afraid of his touch. Away from my father, too, the man who—as I was leaving—was already leaning down, scooping the money off the ground and shoving it into his pockets.

I left all of that behind. But the shame that tore at my insides like razor blades and broken glass?

It kept pace.

Chapter 15

That night in my room, I lay in bed, wishing I really could run away. Of course, my butt hurt so bad after Dad had used his belt on it that I probably wouldn't have made it across the yard.

At least I hadn't yelled when he'd done it. Maybe Ernest and Isabelle hadn't heard. I hoped not.

I still couldn't believe he'd whipped me. He threatened to do it all the time, but I hadn't been punished that way since I hit my growth spurt. Heck, even the other kids in my grade who weren't big like me didn't get whippings anymore. It was all about taking away their video games or cell phones. Of course, I didn't have any of that, so maybe this was all Dad could think of.

I could have stopped him, I knew. "Lean over," he'd said, and I'd done it, staring at the worn seat on the sofa as I waited for the first blow to fall. I was almost as tall as he was, and faster on foot. I could have gotten away, probably. But I hadn't even tried.

I deserved to get beat for what I'd done.

I just wished I could return the favor, for what my dad did—taking that money from Mr. King—no, worse than taking it. He'd scraped it off his lawn like a dog with scraps, grateful for it.

We'd been poor a long time—pretty much my whole life. I had learned to live with it. But I'd always thought Dad was too proud to do something like that, even though things had gotten worse lately. I guess Dad wasn't proud at all.

I'd learned a lot today, none of it good.

I squeezed my eyes shut, wishing I could sleep. Instead, I heard my mom's voice, quiet and low in the next room. "You were awful hard on the boy. You could have hurt him."

"Huh," Dad said. I heard a clink. He was drinking again—Jack Daniels. He'd stopped at the liquor store after he'd picked me up on the road, and spent twenty bucks of Mr. King's money on booze. I wondered if it was possible to drink enough to forget what he'd done. "Boy, nothing. He's the size of a man. And he had it coming."

"He's still a boy, John," Mom said, softer. "What could have made him go off like that, anyway? Why would he say such things to Mr. King?"

A silence, then Dad answered her. Lying. "I got no idea."

My gut burned. I hadn't been allowed to say my side of the

story to Mom, hadn't been allowed to talk. Dad had threatened me with worse than a whipping if I said anything to set Mom off. He was probably right; she was having so many bad days now, the slightest thing could send her into a state, rocking and crying for hours.

But it hurt, her thinking I'd just been acting crazy.

"Did you say Mr. King paid you extra?" Mom said, changing the subject. "That's good. The landlord came by today while you were gone. I tried to pay him some of it, but he said no. All or nothing, John. He said he had somebody else who wanted to live here. Said we couldn't have any extra days this month, after the last two. He needs it Friday."

"You tell him he'll get it Friday," Dad said. "We got enough for rent right now, just about six hundred dollars total with what I got today. Mr. King pays me for the week, we'll have enough for rent *and* the rest of the bills."

I knew what Mom was thinking as well as he did. She was trying to find a way to ask Dad to give her the money, so we'd have it safe at home instead of in his pocket and at the liquor store. But she didn't have to say anything.

"Don't worry," he said. "I'll give you the money in the morning." Mom's relieved sigh was punctuated by the clink of Dad's ice cubes.

I wanted to burst in on them and demand the money back. I was going to take those bills and stuff every single one down

Mr. King's throat until he turned purple and died. I'd had a long time to think about Gayle, and how she'd looked. How she'd sounded sitting up in her nest. Broken.

She'd sounded like he'd broken something in her.

But the next morning, I wasn't allowed to go to work. I was waiting in the truck cab when Dad climbed in. He didn't look at me. "Get out," he said.

"I'm coming today," I said.

"No, you're not," he repeated. "Get out of the truck."

If I didn't come with him, how could I check on Gayle? It was almost five miles out to Mr. King's. I had to find a way to get him to take me over. "You can't cut that sycamore limb by yourself."

"I can, and I will," he said, gripping the steering wheel hard. "You insulted the man who's paying me, and he told me not to bring you back over. You're not welcome."

"But Gayle—" I tried.

Dad cut me off. "Leave her alone."

"But she needs me," I yelled.

"Needs you?" He narrowed his eyes and said each word slowly. "Haven't you done enough?" He shook his head. "Get out."

I opened the door and climbed out. The door hadn't even shut all the way when my legs were peppered by flying bits of gravel, and my face covered by a cloud of exhaust and dust.

I choked, but I didn't think it was from the dust.

I wandered back inside, feeling my throat close up. Wondering what was happening to Gayle. Imagining my dad going out to Mr. King's, smiling and laughing with him. Laughing at me, the dumb kid who couldn't keep his cool.

I opened the front door and heard Mom in the rear of the house, humming. "Mom? Where are you?" I walked toward her. Maybe, if she was having a good day, I could help her out. I knew she wasn't going to be cooking much; there wasn't a lot left in the pantry. Some oatmeal, and a few cans of milk and corn. Maybe we could go to the church and help sort the food pantry. Lots of times, there were cans of stuff just past the expiration date, and the pastor let volunteers take them home. He said it was "hurtful to the dignity of the people who came to get food" to have to take expired cans.

I remember wondering what that must be like—to have so much dignity, you wouldn't want perfectly good green beans on your plate.

Maybe there would be tuna fish.

"Mom?" I yelled again, but softer. "Where are you?"

"Folding clothes," she called back. "Come on in. You can help put them away."

I thought she was in my room, but she wasn't. She was sitting on Raelynn's bed, pulling a bunch of her old shirts out of a basket, one at a time, and folding them up. The pile of hair ribbons was hanging out of her pocket, and they looked freshly ironed. She'd been working on Raelynn's stuff for a while, I supposed. Maybe she hadn't even slept.

"Mom," I said softly, worried. Was this what she did every day when Dad and I were out? "Mom, why did you wash Raelynn's clothes?"

"Little John, what a question!" She swatted me on the arm softly as I sat down. "You know how dirty she gets. She's all tomboy, that one. Probably because she loves you so much. You know," Mom said, her face creasing with a thoughtful smile, "she'd follow you anywhere." She laughed once. "If you jumped off a cliff, she'd probably—if you jumped—jumped . . ." She'd remembered.

She crumpled on the bed, wailing.

"Mom, stop!" I yelled and jumped up. I knew I shouldn't— I knew it would set her off even worse, but I couldn't listen. She'd seen Raelynn fall—Dad had seen it, too. We'd all been out in the yard that day. I'd hoped Mom had forgotten exactly how it had all happened, since she'd never mentioned it. But she'd remembered, I could tell. Her eyes filled with tears and blame, looking at me. "Why'd you do it, Little John? Why'd you have to go and jump out of that tree, show her that? Didn't you know she always had to do what you did?"

"I know," I croaked out. "I wasn't trying to do anything wrong, Mom. I didn't know—"

"You should have. Why can't you do what's right?"

What's right? I knew what was right. What was right was to take that money and stuff it down Mr. King's throat. To demand that he apologize to Gayle.

What was right would be if my mother knew who I was, could forgive me for what had happened. Or could forget.

At the very least, a mom who still loved me, even though I hadn't been able to save my sister.

But one thing I'd learned in the past ten months was this: What was *right* didn't have a thing to do with what *was*.

I tried anyway. "Momma, you don't mean that."

Mom stood up, and the ribbons slipped out of her pocket to form a messy heap on the floor. "Get out of here, now," she said.

I stood, feeling the hot tears slip down my face, feeling my heart beat so loud, I couldn't think over the sound. Couldn't breathe.

"Here," I said, picking up the hair ribbons. "Here's her ribbons."

But Mom wouldn't look at me. She just turned her head away and said, "Go." So I went. But right before I left the house, I took a detour. I went into her room, pulled the secret metal box out from underneath her dresser—Mom's special hiding place I'd discovered with Ernest when we were six—and found the money, all five hundred filthy dollars of it.

It folded and fit into my pocket perfectly. I took it and went to do what was right.

Chapter 16

At first, I ran too fast and got winded. Then I paced myself. Our house was a ways into the center of town, and I couldn't afford to get tired too quick. The heat poured over everything like sap, sticking my shirt to my back and my hair to my scalp.

The grass in the lawns I ran past was dry and yellow this late in July, and the whole area hummed with cicadas and air-conditioner units cooling off the people inside the houses.

I ran past the church, the post office, and slowed down as I approached the only other store on the street: the Emperor's Emporium.

It was the first one he'd built, and the biggest. Part of the logo was a giant crown on a head that looked a little like Mr. King's. I wanted to put a rock through the window, right there, where his head was.

Why not? I thought. I'd never done anything like that before, but there wasn't anyone to stop me. Was there?

I looked around. The street was empty, except for a black dog sniffing the curb a few blocks away. There, right in front of me, was a rock. I picked it up, wondering at how perfectly it fit in my hand. Like someone had left it there for me to find, to throw. I pulled my arm back, ready to let go right at the Emperor's smiling face, when I heard a shop-door bell. Someone was coming out of the Emporium.

"Little John?"

"Isabelle?" I lowered my arm. It was her. But why was she alone? "What are you doing here?" I asked, stuffing the rock in my pocket.

"I was looking for a birthday present for Ernest," she said, lisping the S sounds. "It's his birthday tomorrow, remember?"

"Oh, yeah." Ernest had a summer birthday. It meant he was one of the youngest kids in the class. Up to that year, it also meant he was about the same size as me—what with me being a runt, and him being so young—but then I grew.

"Are you going to come over to the party?" she said, eyes darting back to the store. Ernest must be in there, I realized. "You gave us that dead bird and all. I told him that meant we were all still friends. He is your best friend still, right?"

My cheeks burned. "I wasn't invited," I said. "I guess my 'best friend' Ernest forgot." The words sounded mean, even to me. I knew it wasn't Ernest's fault at all that we weren't friends anymore, but I didn't care. I felt like being mean, like blaming someone else for once. I turned to run off, but a hand on my arm stopped me.

"No," she said, her gray eyes wide. "He didn't forget. He told your momma twice to tell you. Didn't she say?"

"Say what?"

"You're invited. He only got to invite four kids this year. You were the first name on the list." She chewed her lip. "He came over three times last week, but you weren't home. He said you didn't like us no more. But then you were nice to me at church, even though you didn't say yes to Ernest about the party . . ."

Last week I had been working at Mr. King's. Ernest had come over. Three times. "Mom knew? Are you sure?" Isabelle's mouth turned down at the corners.

"I went over with him once. She said she'd tell you." She paused. "But she wasn't . . . feeling very well that day. She kept trying to get me to play with . . . with . . ." She tucked her head down.

"With Raelynn?" I finished softly. Isabelle nodded. I swallowed the hot knot of fear and shame swelling up inside. I thought Mom had been able to hide it from everyone but Dad and me. But if Isabelle knew . . . the whole town probably did.

The knot grew bigger as anger started to balloon in my stomach. I'd given up everything—even my best friend—to keep my family's secrets. And it turned out that maybe there hadn't been a secret to keep.

Maybe it had all been for nothing. I felt like screaming, and I guess Isabelle noticed, since she backed up a step, concern in her eyes. It was time to change the subject. I faked a smile. "Did you find a present for Ernie, then?"

She wiped her face with one arm, nodded, and pulled something small out of her pocket.

It was a lump of paper wrapped around something no bigger than a Matchbox car. She unwrapped the paper to show me what it was: a tiny, hand-painted metal truck. "An ambulance?" I guessed.

"Yep," she said.

"It's perfect. He's gonna love it."

She smiled up at me. "I'll get you one for your birthday if you want. If you're not too big for toys."

"Thanks," I managed. "I'm not too big. Not really." I sort of wanted to hug her, but two more people walked out of the Emporium just then. Ladies from church, Trudy Lester and another lady, part of Mom's prayer circle. They waved, and I waved back.

Once they'd walked off, I put my hand back in my pocket, feeling the rock. It had been stupid, thinking of throwing it here. There were so many people who'd see—even if I hadn't known they were there.

"I gotta go," Isabelle said. "Ernest is at the 7-Eleven. You wanna go say hi?"

"Nah," I said, trying to look like I didn't care. "You tell him . . . tell him happy birthday for me, okay?" *Tell him I didn't know he'd invited me,* I wanted to say. But I couldn't do that to Mom.

"Okay," Isabelle said, that sad, grown-up look back in her eyes again. "You can still come to the party, you know. If you want to. Or just come over." She paused, waiting. I didn't know what to say.

"It got dug up after all," she said at last.

"What?"

"The baby bird. Something dug it up."

"Oh, sorry," I said. "That happens."

"Not when you help," she disagreed, her pale eyebrows furrowing. "You're the best hole digger, Little John. Next time, tell your daddy you need to come over and help. Okay?"

"Okay," I agreed when she scowled at me. "I will . . . if I can."

"Good." She wrapped the ambulance back up and walked down the sidewalk.

I watched her go. She was the same as ever. Spunky, demanding. Bossy where Raelynn had been sweet. Ernest had said they were a perfect match, with no more sense between them than a box full of geese. Ernest was always coming up with stuff like that.

I missed him so bad. I wanted nothing more than to go with Isabelle to the 7-Eleven and meet up with him. Maybe spend the day with both of them. But I couldn't.

I had a different little girl I had to take care of.

I glanced back at the window to the Emporium, the anger starting to churn around inside me again. The eyes in the painting seemed to follow Isabelle. It made me want to smash them out even more.

Then, all of a sudden, with my fingers gripping the rock in my pocket so hard I could feel it cutting into my skin, I knew that smashing out the eyes of the window wouldn't be enough.

I wouldn't be satisfied until I'd thrown the money back at his feet. And then thrown the sharpest rock I could find at his face.

Luckily for me, I knew where he lived. I started running again.

I stopped twice for water, drinking from the outside taps by two houses I'd never been in before, although I recognized the cars from the church parking lot. I didn't bother to ask for a cup, or permission to use the taps; I was too set on getting to Mr. King's before I could change my mind about the whole thing.

I had never run this many miles before, not all at once. In gym class at school, they had us do two miles sometimes, and once a year a 5K, but never five miles. It felt good, though, the warm air pushing into my lungs and hissing out with each breath, the pad of my sneakers on the asphalt.

It would have been relaxing if it hadn't been for the thoughts that kept running through my head. I still didn't know what had happened to Gayle. She hadn't been able to speak. Had he done something to her throat? Her voice itself?

Maybe . . . maybe I should go to her house—well, her tree—and find out, before I went over to Mr. King's.

It would be good to know what I was smashing in his face for, exactly.

I was almost there, almost to the Cutlins', when the ambulance came up behind me. The driver beeped the siren to get me to run on the shoulder. I moved over, wondering where they were going. There weren't any other houses out on this side of town, and the hospital was in the other direction.

Maybe, I thought kicking viciously at a stone that came up in front of me as I ran, maybe it was Mr. King. Maybe he'd had a heart attack or something. A stroke, like my grandma had had.

I hoped so.

Then I was almost there. I could see the Cutlins' fence, and the ambulance. It had stopped right on the side of their house, not at Mr. King's at all.

Who was hurt? My heart, already pounding from the run, skipped a beat when I saw where the paramedics were running.

"No!" I whispered, and picked up the pace, my feet pounding faster than my heart.

They were heading for the sycamore tree.

I knew what had happened. I knew it, deep down.

Gayle had fallen.

And for the second time in my life, I hadn't been there to save her.

Chapter 17

Jebediah Cutlin and his mom were standing on the grass in the front yard, looking toward the back like they were spectators at some sort of game. I ran past, but Jeb's hand shot out and grabbed my shirt, ripping it at the shoulder. "Stop," he shouted, as I tore free from his grasp. "They said to stay back!"

"The heck with that," I yelled. Maybe there was something I could do—even if it was just to apologize. If she was still alive, that was.

I ran around the back to where the paramedics were working on a figure on the ground. As I got closer, though, something tried to click in my mind.

Something wasn't right. There was no pink-and-brown plaid shirt, no brown hair spread out on last year's leaves.

Instead, through the gaps I could see around the men working frantically, there was a blue work shirt, stained with blood. A pair of long legs in blue jeans.

A pair of brown leather work boots I knew well, since they sat right outside my own front door every evening.

"Dad!" I yelled, and stepped forward. But one of the paramedics turned his head and barked out an order.

"Stay back, son," he said. "We've got to get him on the stretcher. Move back now. Move!" I obeyed, my body shuffling back. My brain was filled with the humming of hundreds of wasps. The two men hefted Dad—"one, two, three"—onto a stretcher on the ground next to him. They had tied something around one of his arms . . . or what was left of his arm.

His arm wasn't just broken, I saw. Below the elbow, it was bandaged and wrapped so thickly I couldn't tell what had happened. Was it cut up?

Was it . . . missing?

The paramedics lifted him and hustled toward the open doors of the ambulance. In seconds, the doors were shut, and I was alone, staring at the splotches of blood on the ground, and a broken branch.

Tiny white pinpricks of light danced in front of my eyes, and I slumped over, dizzy. Maybe I was going to pass out. I felt grass under my seat, prickling through my jeans, and then—a hand on my arm.

"I'm sorry, Little John," Gayle said, whispering the words. "I tried to fix him, but I couldn't."

I closed my eyes, working to breathe slower.

A voice called out from the Cutlins' house. "Little John? I'm calling Pastor Martin for you. You stay put."

"Yes, ma'am," I shouted back automatically. I didn't think I could get up anyway; my legs weren't answering my brain. I felt Gayle lean up against me.

"What happened?" I asked her.

"He was trying to cut the bad limb on my tree. But he couldn't do it—" Her voice trailed off, and I finished the sentence for her.

"Alone?" I pounded my forehead with my palms. I wished I had a hammer, so I could just crush my skull in and have it done with.

"It's not your fault," she said. "I was talking to your dad before he got hurt. He said he made you stay home today." She paused, and took a deep breath. "He asked me about Mr. King."

"Yeah?" I didn't look up, but I listened. "What did you tell him?"

"He said I should stay away from Mr. King," she said. "I told him I was going to." She paused again. "He's a bad man."

Oh, God. What had happened to her?

"I shouldn't have taken you over there. I should have listened to you. I shouldn't have done it, for five hundred dollars or a million. I'm—" My voice broke. "I'm so sorry." But *sorry* wouldn't make it right. How could I make it up to her, repay her for the wrong I'd done?

I had an idea.

Why should I stuff the money down Mr. King's throat? I reached into my pocket and pulled it out, the whole roll. "Here. I want you to have it."

"I don't want it," she said.

For some reason, that made me angry. "Just take it," I said, and shoved it toward her again.

"What for?"

"To buy something?" I pointed up at the tree. "A treasure, maybe. Something shiny."

"Treasures don't come from the store, Little John." She looked disappointed in me, like I should have known that.

"Fine. But it's not right for me to have it. I don't care what you do with it. Use it to—" I looked up into the air. "Use it to line your nest, make it into paper airplanes. But I'm not taking it home." I set it on the ground. The money was the wrong shade of green against the grass, a flat, dead color.

Silence stretched between us, like a vibrating string, tight and pulled close to breaking. Then, slowly, she picked up the money and tucked it into one hand. It was a thick roll, and she couldn't quite wrap her fingers around it. "I'll put it in my nest, then," she said.

"Fine." Somewhere, far away, a mockingbird began to trill,

changing songs every few seconds, like he couldn't decide which song was his. Gayle sniffled, and wiped her runny nose with the wad of cash.

"I couldn't fix your dad," she said at last. "I can't fix anything now."

"Sure you can," I said. I knew she thought her voice had powers. I wasn't going to be the one to tell her that was just a story she'd made up, the kind of thing little girls liked to think. I wasn't going to steal anything else from Gayle.

"No, you don't get it. Mr. King stole it."

"Stole what?"

"My voice."

"What do you mean?" I didn't understand.

"What he did," she whispered. "He disappeared my voice. He took it. I didn't know anybody could do that. Why anybody would. And now it's gone.

"Watch." There was a moth on the ground, one that must have gotten caught under a falling branch. One of its wings was bent, and it lay there, on her palm, like a thrown-away kite. She opened her mouth and took a breath. I waited for the notes to come out, the melody that—even if I didn't know if it could really heal things—had made my heart feel whole and happy every time I'd heard it, and was so much a part of her.

But no melody came out. Just a thready wisp of air, rattling, like the last breath of a dying animal.

"See?" She waited for me to look at the moth. She shook her hand. The moth flapped there, uselessly beating its good wing in an attempt to fly away.

For a moment, I just stared at the moth, wondering what she meant. Did she really think she could save a moth with a broken wing?

"You know you can't save everything, right?" I said at last. I put my hand out for the moth and took it, setting it on a piece of broken branch. "You can't . . . really fix all the hurt things in the world. That's not your job, Gayle."

She sighed, that broken sound again. "I know it's not."

"Okay," I said, and stood up. I had to go. Go make sure Mrs. Cutlin had called Mom, make sure someone could take her and me to the hospital.

Make sure Dad was okay.

But I heard Gayle's voice as I left, five words that stayed with me the rest of that week.

"It's not your job either."

Chapter 18

The hospital in Brownwood smelled like lemon cleaner and antiseptic, the kinds of smells that practically stripped your nose clean from the inside. I took a deep breath anyway and followed Pastor Martin through the set of doors marked INTENSIVE CARE.

Verlie Cutlin had called Mom to let her know what was going on, but she hadn't been home, since it was the day she helped stock the food pantry. Somehow Ernest's mom had already heard—probably one of the other neighbors had been listening to the police scanner again—and she'd brought Mom in. Ernest had answered the phone at my house—which was weird, but helpful, I supposed. Pastor Martin came out to pick me up from the Cutlins' house, along with something for us to eat while we waited to hear about Dad.

The smell of fried chicken wafted out of the bag I was

holding under my arm, and my stomach growled. I hadn't eaten breakfast or lunch, I'd run a long way, and I wasn't sure I was going to be able to wait much longer.

A nurse stopped us at the door to the ICU. "I'm sorry," she said to the pastor. "Only two visitors per room. His wife is already in there with him."

"How is he doing, Arlene?" Pastor Martin asked, quietly, with a sideways glance at me. I tried to act like I couldn't hear them and wasn't paying attention. But I listened hard when the nurse answered.

"His arm is pretty bad. But the doctor thinks he'll keep it."

"Thank God," I muttered and slumped against the wall.

Pastor Martin looked like he wanted to say the same thing, but he just nodded at me. "This is the son."

The nurse cleared her throat and frowned at me, then straightened up. "Son, you wait here. I'll tell your mother where you are." She motioned to a chair and waved Pastor Martin inside.

I sat there for what seemed like hours. When the door opened, Mom stepped out. I jumped up, knocking the bag of fried chicken to the floor. "How is he?"

Mom smiled at me, but her face was twitching, like it couldn't decide whether to let her make the expression. "Well, he's out of the woods, they say." She sank down on the chair beside me. "He's sleeping now."

"Can I—can I see him?"

"I don't know," she said, chewing at her lower lip. "I think it might be better to wait."

"Just for a minute," I said. I had to get the picture of him all torn up, lying at the bottom of the sycamore, out of my head. I had to try to tell him I was sorry for leaving him alone, even though he'd told me to stay home. He and I both knew that job had been too big for one man. If I'd put it to him that way, if I'd been thinking of him and not my own troubles, and Gayle's . . .

I had to apologize for not being there to help him.

Mom just nodded. "Don't wake him."

The nurse looked like she wasn't going to let me in at first. But Pastor Martin came out and waved me in as he left, probably in a hurry to eat the fried chicken. I could hear his stomach grumbling as he walked by.

Dad's room had a glass door and a curtain that hid most of him from view. I stepped behind it. He was hooked up to so many tubes, I couldn't keep track of where they came from and where they went. He had tubes in both arms, and a mask over his face for oxygen or something. The machines next to him beeped softly and hissed, like sleeping snakes.

Dad looked smaller and pale. There were scratches all down his face and neck, probably where small branches had hit him when the larger one fell. His arm—I made myself look at it. It wasn't that bad, from what I could tell. Of course, it was wrapped up in so many bandages, I couldn't see much. But it looked the right length. Like maybe there was still an arm under there, after all.

"I'm sorry, Dad," I breathed. "I won't ever let you down again."

Of course, he didn't answer. But the beep and hiss of the machines sounded like a recording machine that was keeping track of my promise. I knew this was a promise I had to keep.

I heard Mom talking to Pastor Martin as I left the ICU wing.

"No," she said softly, "we don't need money. Mr. King called the hospital and said he'd pay the bill here. And for the work John had done up to today."

But what about next week, next month? I wondered.

"You know we'll be here for you, Mary," Pastor Martin said. "Just call."

"Thank you." Mom stood up, catching sight of me at last. "But we'll manage. We had a little windfall this week, so we can make rent."

I felt cold sweat break out on the back of my neck. The money. The five hundred dollars. Mom thought it was at home, and the landlord was coming tomorrow.

The fried chicken I'd eaten, waiting for Mom to come out of the ICU, flipped around in my stomach like it had grown feathers and was planning to fly up my throat.

Mom wandered off to speak to the nurse one more time.

Pastor Martin came over to me, rested his hand on my shoulder. "I know it's hard, son, but you'll have to be the man of the house for a while. Think you can handle that?"

I nodded, wondering what that even meant. Was I supposed to start drinking Jack Daniels and watching the news?

Pastor Martin saw my confusion. "Just help out a bit more. Keep an eye on your mom." He leaned down, whispered into my ear with breath that smelled like drumsticks. "She's a little . . . upset, right now. Keeps talking about your sister. Like she's still alive. Has she been doing that . . . before today?"

"No, sir," I lied.

"Oh," he said, shifting his feet, and his eyes. "That's good, then. I'll tell the doctor. She had him a little worried in there. Thought he might have to check her in for some . . . extra care. He thinks it best she goes home now, with you. Pack some things for the next few days, and get some rest." He leaned back, looked me in the eyes. "You let me know if she needs help. Okay?"

I nodded again, and Pastor Martin straightened up as Mom approached. He smiled at both of us. "Now, I'm going to take you two home, and I'll pick your mom back up in the morning. Can you stay home tomorrow, hold down the fort?"

"Sure," I said. "I'll hold it down."

I did as I was told. I held down the fort—which meant re-heating the casseroles that Mom's church circle had brought over and put in the fridge, feeding the cat, and cleaning the dishes—until Mom went to sit, TV on, in the living room recliner.

I held down the fort until she fell asleep there. But then?

I'm pretty sure only the whip-poor-will calling outside my window heard me bawling through the night. And that was the only good thing I could say about the whole day.

Chapter 19

The next two days we spent in the hospital, waiting for doctors to come and talk to us. Waiting for nurses to ask Mom to sign more papers. Waiting to find out if Dad was coming home anytime soon.

Nothing had changed, except that my stomach hurt every time I thought about the money.

How were we going to pay rent? I'd thought about asking Pastor Martin for it, but didn't. He wouldn't understand any of it.

A sick twist in my gut told me what I'd have to do, where I'd have to go to get the money back, but I didn't want to think about that. Not yet. It felt like breaking another promise.

Friday morning came. It was a good day for Mom, which surprised me. I'd expected her to get more upset. But the women in her circle had been coming by the hospital, coming by the house, too, to check on the cat and water the plants. They'd filled the pantry with food, and the fridge with Jell-O casseroles. It had cheered Mom up, even though Dad was still in bad shape.

I got up, and breakfast—oatmeal with sugar in it, and a glass of milk—was waiting for me at the table. "Mom?" I asked. Her eyes were ringed by dark circles, and her hair was wild. But she smiled at me. She even came over and patted me on the shoulder.

"Sweetheart, there you are! I thought you were going to sleep the day away!"

"Are you—okay, Mom?"

She patted me once more and moved back to the sink. "What a question. With your father hurt like he is? All right." She sighed and went back to washing the dishes that had been piling up for two days. "Now you need to get dressed," she said.

"Are we going to the hospital?" She shook her head.

"I need you to stay here today," she said. "Pastor called a few minutes ago. Said he was coming by in a half hour to take me back to Brownwood. There! I'm done." She pulled off her apron, catching her hair in the pocket button. I stepped across the floor to help untangle it, but she waved me off. "No, no," she said. "I've got it. I just need you to"—and she yanked so hard on the knot of hair, I saw several strands tear free of her scalp—"stay here and give the landlord the rent money. You can do that, can't you?"

I was glad she wasn't looking at me right then—I knew for a fact I was showing what I felt on my face. Horror, panic, guilt. But Mom was busy hanging up her apron.

"Yeah, I can," I said.

"Fine," she answered, on her way to her bedroom. "I'll get the money for you, then. Make sure you get a receipt from him," she called back.

I raced after her. "No, Mom, it's okay. I can get the money."

"No, you can't," she answered. "It's hidden."

I couldn't actually call out that I knew where her hiding place was. But then I saw someone walking up our sidewalk. It was Pastor Martin. "Mom!" I yelled. "Pastor's here! He looks like he's in a hurry, too!"

Which wasn't exactly true, but it got her out of the bedroom. "Oh, no!" she called. "Is it nine o'clock already?" She pushed her hair back from her face, the money completely forgotten.

I shepherded her toward the front door, and she opened it. "Pastor Martin, won't you come inside?"

"No," he said. "I'm so sorry I had to come a bit early. A homebound parishioner is dying, poor soul. You may remember Mrs. Davis? She hasn't been to church in years, after her fall. I got a call this morning. So I'll need to take you now, if that's okay?"

"Oh, yes," she said. She turned back to me, distracted. She leaned close for a hug, I thought. But it was just to tell me about the money. "The rent is in a box under my chest of drawers. He gets six hundred dollars, not a penny more." She called out again as she followed Pastor Martin to his car, "And get a receipt!"

I went to the box first, to see how much money there was left. I remembered seeing some other bills. Was it possible there was still six hundred dollars there?

There wasn't, of course. If there had been, Mom would have paid the landlord before now. There were four twenty-dollar bills, two tens, and a bunch of change.

There was nothing for it. I knew what I had to do, even if it was awful to think about. I grabbed a handful of the change and stuffed it in my pocket. Then I stuck the twenties and tens into an envelope and tacked it to the front door for the landlord. It wouldn't be enough, though. Wouldn't keep us from getting evicted. I was going to have to go back over to the Cutlins' and get the rest of the rent money back out of Gayle's nest.

She hadn't really cared about it, I told myself, as I put my shoes on and got ready to run the ten-mile round trip. She didn't care about money. What was it she had put in her nest? Treasures, she'd said.

Maybe I could trade her something! But what would an eight-year-old girl treasure?

It was so obvious, I felt stupid. I ran into Raelynn's room and grabbed up the one thing I knew for a fact Gayle would love—

and I knew she didn't have. Her hair ribbons. Then I started running.

I stopped for a minute at the 7-Eleven to soak in a little air-conditioning. The girl behind the counter frowned and asked me what I was planning to buy. "A Coke," I said, like I had been planning that all along. I had just enough change left over—if I used the three pennies from the dish by the cash register—for a piece of gum for Gayle. The girl frowned at me again when I scooped up the pennies, but then smiled when I told her the gum was for the Cutlins' foster girl.

I ran on, my feet feeling the soreness from my run the day before. My tennis shoes were getting tight again. Was I still growing? I hoped not; shoes were expensive.

A mile or so out of town, I passed the black dog that had been hanging around the Emperor's house. I pitched a rock at it, just to keep it from following. It slunk off into the brush, but I could feel its eyes on me for a long time after.

When I got to the Cutlins' front yard, I stopped. I could hear Gayle singing, as clear as day. It wasn't the best I'd ever heard her sound—her voice seemed a little trembly, and she was singing awfully loud. She usually made sure to sing softer in the Cutlins' yard. "Gayle?" I yelled out. The front door opened.

"What are you here for?" Jeb Cutlin had on a pair of running shorts and a shirt I'd seen in the church donation box. I knew, because it was one I'd worn the previous year and outgrown before it got old-looking. It made me feel better, knowing I wasn't the only one in town whose mom did some of her clothes shopping from the donation box. And knowing Jeb couldn't tease Gayle for wearing old hand-me-down clothes, since he was wearing them, too? That almost made me smile.

Jeb caught me looking at his shirt. He looked down and flushed red. Maybe he remembered it had been my shirt, too.

"What do you want?" he asked again. "Why aren't you at the hospital with your folks?"

I wasn't about to tell him I was here to get the money out of Gayle's nest. So I just shrugged. "I got something for Ga—Suzie."

"Ga-Suzie?" he repeated, stepping closer. His voice got softer, and he looked back at the house. I wasn't sure, but something in his eyes looked familiar, like the same thing I'd been feeling all day, all week—guilty. "What do you got there? Maybe you should give it to me. I'll give it to her for ya."

Sure he would. I pulled the ribbons out of my pocket. "Girl stuff," I said. "I didn't think you'd want them, you not being a little girl." I gave him a look that said I thought he was exactly that. He flushed even redder and looked like he wanted to pound me, but he held back. I kept teasing him. "But you know, Jeb, this blue one would just match your eyes." I held out one ribbon, stepped toward him like I was going to put it in his hair for him.

"Go to—" The screen door slammed on the last word, but I knew what he'd said. I didn't care. With him gone, I could run around the back of the house and talk to Gayle. I could still hear her singing, loud as could be.

She'd gotten her voice back. I smiled. At least one good thing had happened today.

But when I got to the backyard, the singing stopped. "Gayle?" I called.

The singing started back up, the same song. It wasn't coming from the Cutlins' at all, I realized. And it wasn't Gayle singing—I'd never heard her sing the same song twice, and not in that shaky voice.

It was a recording.

I ran to the fence and looked over. The Emperor had his windows open, the curtains blowing in and out with the breeze, and he was listening to the recording of Gayle he had made. I scanned his garden and the Cutlins' yard.

Gayle wasn't there. I looked up, into the sycamore tree. "Gayle?" I called, but I saw immediately that Gayle wasn't there. She couldn't be there.

Because her nest was gone.

Chapter 20

W here was it?

There was nothing left in the limbs of the sycamore, noth-ing to show there had ever been a nest to begin with. I scanned the ground for traces of it and found them, though. A candy wrapper—the silver one I'd given her, I thought. And some pebbles? I leaned down and picked up one. It had a streak of quartz running straight through the middle, a jagged line that looked like a hatching egg. I gathered up what I could find— mostly bits of paper that had words written on them in eight-year-old handwriting. Had it been a letter? I could only make out a few words—*Mom* and *song* and *miss*. I stuffed everything I could—the candy wrappers, the papers, and even the peb-bles—in my pocket.

A fluttering by the fence made me realize the breeze had caught something else. When I got there, I realized it was—

hair? Long hairs, twining around the rough wood of the fence posts. I gathered it up and rubbed it between my fingers. I knew the softness. It was the same downy feeling of the baby swallow I'd picked up outside the garage. It was Gayle's hair. Had she pulled it out to make a soft place in her nest?

She'd always had such a tangled mess up there, underneath all her flower crowns, I wouldn't have known if she was missing a patch or two.

But there was so much, I realized. It was blowing all around the yard. Had she cut her hair?

I remembered Raelynn cutting her hair in kindergarten, coming home to Mom, who was madder than a wet hen. Not because her hair looked terrible, but because Raelynn had cut the softest part of her hair the shortest—the curls that gathered at the base of her neck. Turns out a little boy had been teasing her, calling her "piggy with a curly tail."

I knew why Mom had cried; Raelynn's hair had been beautiful, softer than anything. As soft as dandelion fluff, as flower petals.

Just as soft as Gayle's hair.

"Gayle?" I yelled. "Gayle, where are you?" Had she run off? The music next door stopped at my voice, then started again.

The back door of the Cutlins' house opened up, though. Verlie Cutlin stepped out. She was wearing an apron, wringing her hands like she couldn't stop. "What are you back here for, boy? You get on home now."

"Where's Gayle?" I demanded, marching toward the house. Mrs. Cutlin took a step back, then scowled at me. I didn't care if she was afraid. She should be. I wanted nothing more than to hit something, someone. Hurt whoever had taken down the nest.

"Where's who?" She spat to one side.

"Suzie. Where's Suzie?"

"None of your business," Mrs. Cutlin said, her eyes going so squinty I couldn't see the whites at all. "You got no business here." She moved to block the doorway. What was she hiding? Had she been hurting Gayle? Had she and her miserable kid laid hands on that little girl? Mrs. Cutlin gasped and took another step back; I wondered what my face looked like.

"I'll call the police," she blustered.

"I'll go once I see her," I said, trying to calm down. Ticking off Mrs. Cutlin wouldn't do Gayle a lick of good. "Just call her out here."

Mrs. Cutlin looked like she was going to spit again, this time at me, but she didn't. "Fine." She hollered over her shoulder, "Suzie! Suzie. Get on out here."

We waited there for ten, twenty, thirty seconds. The sound of Gayle's recording started up next door again. I could tell Mrs. Cutlin didn't like hearing it. I didn't, either. She was just about to call out for Gayle again when the screen door behind her squealed.

"Oh, God," I said. "What happened?"

"She did it," Mrs. Cutlin said, her voice defensive. "With her own hands. I don't even let my fosters have scissors. She did it herself." She shook her head. "I don't know what I'm gonna tell the caseworker. Girl's crazy. Just look at her."

Gayle looked terrible. Of course, all I could see was the top of her head. The strands of hair in my hand dropped to the ground. She hadn't cut her hair, I could see that now. She had pulled it out. The top of her head was missing great patches of hair, like a dog with mange.

My tongue felt stuck to the roof of my mouth. I couldn't speak, didn't know if I'd be able to force words out, through the shock of seeing her like this.

Gayle's scalp was red and scraped in places, almost bleeding. She'd torn at it so hard she'd almost taken the skin with the hair. For a moment I was reminded of the fawn in the fence. How long had Gayle been like this? Hours? All night?

It had to have taken her some time to do this much damage. It had to have hurt terribly.

I kneeled down to see her face. "Gayle? What'd you do?" She looked up at me, not even trying to smile. Her eyes moved slowly over to the ground where the remains of her nest lay. "What happened to your nest?" I asked, softer. "Did it fall down?" *Had she torn it down?*

"Jeb," she whispered.

"Go back inside, girl," Mrs. Cutlin said, and Gayle started to obey.

"I found these," I said, and pulled the leftovers from the nest out of my pocket. "Do you want them?"

She turned back, and stared at my open palm like I had a poisonous snake in it. "No." She shuddered, and shuffled back toward the door.

I guessed she was right. It might have been treasure before, but it was ruined now. Jeb had done that.

"Wait," I said, remembering what I'd come for. Remembering and realizing at the same time what had happened. "Did you put—what I gave you yesterday—in the nest?"

Gayle didn't turn back, but she nodded once before she shuffled inside.

Then I knew what had happened, and why. It wasn't Jeb's fault, not really. It was mine. I had given her the money in plain sight. Jeb must have seen me do it, and then gone up into her nest to take it.

A kid his size would never have fit in her nest. He broke it up. I couldn't even blame him—if someone had put five hundred dollars in my yard, I'd have climbed the tree, too, if I hadn't been too scared.

It might as well have been me. I was responsible.

And now I was responsible for getting the money back.

If I'd eaten anything for breakfast, I would have thrown it

up. I walked back around to the front of the house and knocked on the door.

I shouldn't have bothered.

Mrs. Cutlin came out, madder than before. "I told you to go, boy. I'm calling the police this time. You're being a nuisance."

"I'm sorry, Mrs. Cutlin," I said, trying to shrink down, look smaller, so maybe she would think of me as a kid. "But I left some money here yesterday—"

She cut me off. "Then that was stupid of you, boy. Now get home. I got work."

The screen door slammed in my face, and I backed up a step. I knocked again, louder, but all I heard in answer was the lock sliding into place.

I had to get money for the landlord, and soon.

First, I went to the base of the sycamore and settled the scraps from Gayle's nest there, so she could find them if she changed her mind. Then I started walking back to town, thinking hard. There wasn't anyone in our town with much money—not five hundred dollars for a kid like me, anyway. I could mow lawns, but that meant only twenty-five dollars a yard, and I couldn't do more than a few lawns a day.

I'd had to make my own spending money for so long, I knew how hopeless it was. I'd done it all—sometimes with Ernest, even though he never really needed the money. We'd picked up aluminum cans from the side of the road to sell at the recycling center, collected dewberries from the banks by the railroad tracks and sold them to teachers at school every May. I'd mowed lawns, raked, and walked dogs for anybody who would pay me a dollar.

The problem was, all my friends did the same thing. There just weren't that many lawns in town that weren't already being taken care of. And no real jobs for a twelve-year-old kid.

I walked slowly, though, trying to think of something—anything.

When I got back to the house, my skin burned from the sun and my head ached from thinking. There were two notes on the door. One was from Ernest. I read it quickly. *Come over for dinner. I'll show you my birthday stuff. I'm sorry about your dad—E. P.S. It's pork chops tonight, so please come.*

I almost laughed. Ernest hated pork chops, and I loved them. He would always wait until his mom was out of the room, then switch his whole one for my gnawed-on bone. His mom had a thing about her kids eating everything on their plates.

Right then, I wanted a pork chop more than anything. A pork chop, and a family who ate meals together, and had enough money for meat . . . and doctor's bills.

And rent.

The other note was from the landlord. I tore it down and scanned it while I filled a glass of water.

He'd heard about the accident. He'd taken the money I'd

left, but it wasn't enough. We still had to pay the rest imme-diately. He was coming back with the eviction notice in a few days, if we didn't bring cash or a money order to his office.

I crumpled both notes up and threw them away, burying them deep under the garbage in the kitchen can. The trash was starting to stink.

The fridge was full of casseroles, but I couldn't stand the smell of all that Jell-O and hamburger meat. Maybe later. So I ate the last of the bread—two heel ends wrapped in a bag in the freezer, with some margarine on them—and got to work.

I didn't want Mom coming home to a filthy house. She al-ready had to come home to a son who'd stolen from her. It was the least I could do.

I must have fallen asleep on the sofa. I woke up to Mom's cool hand on my forehead. "You sick, Little John?" she asked. "You're burning up."

"Sunburn." I tried to sit up. She pushed me back down, gently. "No," she said. "Don't get up." She stood and started out of the room.

At the last minute she turned back. "You paid the landlord," she said. It wasn't a question. "Thanks," she said.

I sat up, startled. "What—"

She smiled. "I checked the money box. Thanks." She clicked off the light. "I knew I could count on you. Now sleep."

I could have stopped her, could have told her the truth then.

But I didn't. She looked so tired, old. I hadn't seen her look like that since the week of Raelynn's funeral.

I closed my eyes, bad memories and guilt filling my mind. I tried to sleep, but I kept remembering that saying. "No rest for the wicked," I'd heard the church ladies say sometimes. I hadn't understood it then, but now I did. I'd never thought of myself as wicked before.

But I was a liar, a thief, and—with the way I'd left my dad to work alone—a hair away from being a murderer. I was wicked for sure. Through and through.

I stayed awake with my dark thoughts for a long time.

Chapter 21

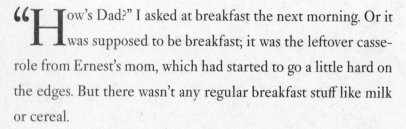

"How's Dad?" I asked at breakfast the next morning. Or it was supposed to be breakfast; it was the leftover casserole from Ernest's mom, which had started to go a little hard on the edges. But there wasn't any regular breakfast stuff like milk or cereal.

I hadn't slept, but I knew I had to do some thinking today, so I was drinking coffee with Mom. She hadn't questioned it when I'd asked—just poured me a cup like it was an everyday thing. The bitterness on my tongue matched what I was feeling inside. Of course, Mom had made extra—she obviously hadn't slept much either.

"He's okay," she said. "Doing better last night, anyway." She closed her eyes for a second, like her head hurt. "The doctor wants to keep him a few more days, but maybe he can come home sooner."

"Really?" Maybe he wasn't that bad. Maybe he would be able to work again, and we could earn the money for the rent after all. I'd work as hard as he needed me to, I knew that.

I had to make this right.

"Are you going back up there today?" I asked. When she nodded, I went on. "Do you want me to come? I was thinking I could mow some lawns, look for a little work?"

She smiled, but the lines between her eyes didn't disappear. "That'd be real good, Little John." She paused, and took a sip of coffee. "We're going to need you to help a lot more, once Dad's home. He's not going to be able to work for weeks."

"Weeks?" I swallowed. The landlord had said he was evicting us in a few days.

"He got cut up pretty bad," she said. "But don't you worry. Pastor Martin said we can get food from the pantry, and once your dad doesn't need me at home, I'll take on some secretarial work they have up there. Fold the bulletins, that sort of thing. If you can do a little more work around town, that'd help. We'll make ends meet."

I fought not to cry or scream. It kept coming back to me— this was all my fault. If I hadn't wanted that money from the Emperor so bad. If Dad hadn't been working alone—I must have said the last few words out loud, because I felt Mom's arms around my shoulders.

"It's not your fault, Little John," she said. "Don't even think that." Her hands were soft on my face, and I leaned into her. It had been so long since she'd held me, I couldn't remember feeling this. Feeling loved.

Even though I didn't deserve it.

She patted me on the shoulder and carried our coffee cups over to the sink to rinse them out. "I have to walk to the church today. The truck is still out at Mr. King's. Pastor said he'll drive me out there so I can take myself to and from the hospital from now on. Sure wish I'd learned to drive a stick shift now," she muttered, and crossed the kitchen. "Can you get lunch together without me?"

"Sure, Mom," I said. I was itching for her to go. I had to have some time alone to think. I guess she could see it in my face.

She smiled again and shook her head. "Look at you, all the worries of the world on that sweet face. Don't be afraid. It could be a lot worse. At least Mr. King's paying all the hospital bills. Of course, he's the only one in town with enough money to do such a thing. So, if this sort of thing had to happen, better there than anywhere else." She turned away. "I'll just go tell Raelynn good-bye."

"Bye, Mom," I whispered. I grabbed a plastic dish of some casserole that smelled like meat loaf, a fork, and a bottle of water from the fridge, tossed them into my backpack, and headed out. I didn't want to see if Mom came out of Raelynn's room crazy or not. I just had to hope for the best.

And try to find work.

• • •

I knocked on fourteen doors, but no one needed any yard work done. Two ladies handed me sodas, and one told me to come back the next week. But the next week would be too late.

I sat in the shade of a soapberry tree and drank the last few swallows of the soda. I was getting desperate. Was this my payback for stealing that ten-dollar bill from the church collection plate, or for all the wrongs I'd done since?

Maybe I needed to ask forgiveness. I got up and headed in the direction of the steeple.

The sanctuary was open, but the church secretary saw me go in. I knew I only had a few minutes to pray before she came in to see what I was up to. I hustled to the front of the church and knelt down.

I didn't pray out loud. In fact, I couldn't pray at all. Only one word came to my mind.

Why?

I thought about it, over and over. Why had all this happened to me, to my mom and dad? We were good people; we'd always tried to do what was right.

Well, Mom had, anyway. I knew I'd done plenty wrong, and Dad? He probably hadn't prayed in . . . longer than I could remember. But it had all started with Raelynn dying.

"Why?" I said out loud. Then louder, "Why?"

"Do you need something, son?" It was Mrs. Haas, the secretary. She hung back at the edge of the sanctuary, like she was afraid to come in—or afraid the phone would ring in her office and she wouldn't hear it. "How's your daddy?"

"Fine, ma'am," I answered, getting up. "I was just . . ."

"Praying?" She smiled, looking at the cross hanging there. "Good. You know, God answers prayer."

I tried not to laugh; I had a feeling it wouldn't be a happy sound. "Well, he hasn't answered mine," I said.

"What is it you were praying for?" she said. "If you can say."

I think she figured I would say "for my dad to be healed," but I didn't. "Money," I stated. "I need five hundred dollars, this week."

"You're not planning on holding up a bank, are you?" She laughed, then stopped, her eyes alarmed. I guess Mr. King had been right about my poker face, since she blurted out, "Don't get any ideas."

I shrugged. Until she said it, I hadn't thought once about stealing the money. Maybe I wasn't such a hopeless sinner after all.

"I don't have any ideas, ma'am," I said. She relaxed.

"I wish I could help you, son. But—" She hesitated. "I don't see why you'd need that much money. Isn't Mr. King paying for your daddy's bills? He's the only one in this town with money to spare." Then the phone rang in her office, and she turned halfway away. I could tell she didn't want to leave me there alone, especially not after she'd seen me consider stealing.

"I'll be right out," I said. "Give me a minute?"

She left, her sandals flapping against the fellowship hall floor.

The only one in town with that much money was the Emperor, she'd said. I felt sick, but I knew what I had to do. Only it seemed like a betrayal of everything I believed in, of the one I'd sworn to take care of, to do it.

"Okay, God. You want this? Send me a sign. Who can help me?" Nothing happened. No bolt of light, no angel choir. So, after a few minutes, I did what Raelynn and I used to do during the most boring sermons. It was time to play Bible fortune-teller. I picked up the Bible in front of me, thumbed through it with my eyes closed, and let the cover fall open on my lap. Without looking, I set my finger on the page.

I opened my eyes and read out loud: "'I found he had done nothing deserving of death, but because he made his appeal to the Emperor . . .'" My voice stopped on the word *Emperor*.

It was as close to a sign as I was going to get.

I dropped the Bible on the pew and got up. As I jogged the rest of the way out to the Emperor's house, I had plenty of time to think. Time to wonder what I was doing.

This was the man who'd scared Gayle so much she couldn't sing. Who'd stolen her voice.

I wanted to kill him.

I had to beg him for money.

Nobody saw, but I stopped twice to throw up meat loaf and soda pop. Whether it was from the running or the thought of what I had to do, I didn't know.

It didn't matter.

Chapter 22

When I got to the Emperor's house, he wasn't there. Dad's truck wasn't, either, which meant Mom had already come by and picked it up. I hoped she hadn't seen me running out this way. Someone was at the house, though. A man in jeans and a long-sleeved shirt was standing by the fence line, shaking his head.

"Excuse me, sir?" I said. "Is Mr. King home?"

"No, son, he's not," the man said. I didn't recognize him, but I knew his name. I'd seen his truck in the driveway. It had a fancy label on it that said DANIEL DEVONSHIRE'S DIAMOND LAND-SCAPES. What worried me, though, was the chain saw and pruning extensions I'd seen in the truck bed.

"Want me to give him a message for you?" he asked.

"No," I said. "I can wait."

"He's not coming back until tomorrow." The man smiled,

trying to be kind, I guessed. But his next words took my breath away. "I can get him a message, though. I'm staying out here, trying to fix the work some idiot did last week." He moved over to examine the cut branch on the sycamore. "Amateur hour," I heard him mutter.

Was he talking about the work Dad had done?

"I don't know what Mr. King was thinking. Must have been doing some poor guy a favor. But this is going to take some work to fix."

My head buzzed. "What do you mean?"

The gardener looked back at me, impatience in his eyes. "Son, I don't have time to talk. If this one's any example, I've got about forty more acres of damage to work on. The last guy who messed with these trees left me plenty to do. Come back tomorrow." He walked off to his truck, pulling his smartphone out of his pocket to call someone.

I wanted to run off, but I remembered what I was there for. My face burning, I called out after him. "You don't need some help, do you? I can haul wood. I'm really strong. And I work cheap."

The man just laughed and waved me off, like I was some sort of stray dog.

I looked at the sycamore. The cuts Dad had made didn't look like the other ones, the ones on the pecans. Obviously, the branch had broken and fallen onto him—or he'd come off his ladder before he'd finished the cut, and the branch had broken then.

It stung, this guy with a fancy phone and a fancy truck, judging my dad by one branch.

The Emperor wasn't home. No one else in town had any money, except for . . .

I knew one family that had money, enough money to pay the rent. The same one who'd taken it. But the Cutlins would never think of giving it back to me. Five hundred dollars was a heck of a lot to people like them, even if they did have cable and AC. And Jeb hated me anyway. He'd be glad to see my family out on the street.

There was no use asking again.

I had to get home. Mom would be back from the hospital before me, at this rate. I tried not to even look at the Cutlins' house as I ran past it.

It was close to six o'clock by the time my feet hit the driveway in front of the house. Uh-oh. Dad's truck was in the driveway. I crossed my fingers that Mom hadn't been home long. "Mom?" I yelled as I ran inside. Maybe she'd made something for dinner—or would at least have some good news about Dad. "How's Dad?" I said, when I pulled open the door.

No one answered, and it took a few seconds for my eyes to adjust to the dim light inside. But when they did, I saw Mom sitting there, on the sofa. Crying. She had something in her hand—a yellow piece of paper. It had been crumpled up, then laid back flat. I could read the words on the top plenty well, even in the dark room. *Notice of Eviction.*

"Mom?" I said. I could feel my heart pounding so hard, the blood pulsed in my neck, my skull, the roof of my dry mouth.

"Mom?" I asked again.

But it wasn't Mom who answered.

"What did you do with the money?"

Chapter 23

"Dad?"

He was lying on the sofa, his head and arm propped up on stacks of pillows. The coffee table had been pulled up alongside the sofa to help support his arm and to make a space for all the bottles of prescription medicines there. There was a soda and a glass of water, sweating rings of condensation onto the fake wood surface.

"How are you, Dad?" I took a step toward him. "I didn't think you'd—"

"Where'd you put the money, boy?" he shouted. Whatever was wrong with his arm obviously hadn't hurt his vocal cords. I jumped at the familiar yell.

I didn't know what to say. How could I explain what I'd done? What could I possibly tell them that would make them understand? I hadn't known how bad we needed the money when I took it. How could I have known there wasn't anything else for the landlord? That Dad wasn't going to be getting any more paychecks from the Emperor?

There was no way the Cutlins would give the money back, and I wasn't about to bring Gayle into this.

There wasn't anybody here who would understand. Who would take my side.

I had to take the blame. "I lost it," I said softly. But each word fell like a grenade into the silence of the room.

I heard a soft moan. Mom was wringing her hands, twisting at the silver ring on her finger—the one that had taken the place of her old gold one, the real one she'd had to sell to afford the down payment on the burial plot for Raelynn. "Where we gonna live?" she murmured, her voice high and strange. "Where we gonna live now?"

"Lost it?" Dad said, then repeated himself, louder. "Lost it where? Lost it at a store? You buy yourself something nice?"

"No," I protested. "Nothing for me. I didn't spend it, not a cent! I just—I lost it."

He could tell I was lying. "Boy," he whispered and started to get up from the sofa. I recognized the gleam in his eye; he was planning to wallop me. But he'd forgotten about his arm, I guess. As soon as he started moving, the pillows shifted, falling to the floor like a block tower, but silently. Dad yelled, "Mary!"

Mom raced over to pick up the pillows. Dad's face was red,

and creased with pain. I knelt down, trying to scoop up the pillows to help, but Dad's growl stopped me.

"Get away from me," he said, each word as clear as a whistle. "Get out of my sight."

I held the pillows out to him, but all he said was "Now!" I set them down at Mom's feet and turned to go.

"Don't . . . come back . . . without . . . that money." His voice followed me out of the house, but I didn't make it far. On the porch, just a few feet away, my legs gave out on me, and my knees folded, until I was sitting on the wood, legs splayed like one of Raelynn's cloth dolls.

Raelynn. Gayle. My parents. I'd let everyone down. I stuffed a fist in my mouth, hoping it would keep the cries from coming out.

I sat there for hours, wondering how to make it right. How could I come up with the money?

The Emperor would be back the next day. If anyone owed us the rent money, it was him.

The night air got cooler. I shifted on the porch, trying not to make a sound. Maybe I could sneak back into my room. But Mom's soft crying and Dad's swearing kept me up most of the night. The moon was brighter than a nightlight, too. After a few hours, I gave up waiting and walked around back, the grass soft under my tennis shoes. I leaned my back up against the stump that had been Raelynn's oak tree. I remembered the day Dad had cut down all the trees in our backyard, the day after the funeral. I had watched, wanting to help. Hating those trees.

Why had Dad left the stump of this one? To remember her by? I knew he'd had plans to burn it out. I ran my fingers along the top of the stump. The chain-saw cuts he'd left had started to weather, get softer. The top was almost smooth, but puckered, like an old scar. I pressed a hand on my chest, wondering if someday the thought of Raelynn would be like that in my heart. Softer, not so sharp.

I didn't know. It seemed like every time I looked up, someone I loved was falling from trees. Was I ever going to get big enough, strong enough, to be able to save them?

Dad had been proud of me, just a few days before. Because I'd acted like a man.

How did a man act, though? I remembered Dad scraping and bowing to Mr. King.

Was that what I had to do, too?

Or was being a man something other than that?

When the sun pinked up the sky across the street, I got to my feet. My muscles were tight and sore, but they loosened up as I walked. Water from the hoses on the way to Mr. King's, and a few pears taken from the tree across the street from the church, and my stomach didn't hurt quite as much.

That is, until I got to Mr. King's house. With my finger on the doorbell, my stomach flipped and slid like a fish on a bank, trying desperately to get back into the water, to escape from the hard gravel-and-sand wrongness of the suffocating ground.

I almost turned away, but Mom's voice echoed in my mind. "Where we gonna live?"

I rang the bell.

Chapter 24

I didn't expect him to answer right away. But before the bell had stopped echoing inside the great house, the door opened. The Emperor stood there, dressed in a bathrobe, a purple one, with a crown embroidered on the pocket.

"Oh, good!" he said. "It's you." He stepped back. "Come in." His eyes darted past me, like he was looking for someone else. My dad?

"Come in," he repeated. "How did you hear?"

What was he talking about? "I'm here about a job," I said slowly, hating each word as it came out. Knowing it was what I had to do, to say, for my family. "I need some money. I'm willing to work."

He hesitated. "Work? What kind of work?"

"Gardening," I said, wondering what he was going on about. His eyes looked red, bloodshot. Almost like he'd been crying.

He waved me into his front hallway, and I smelled something strange. The smell of burning plastic and wiring.

"Mr. King?" I said. "Do you have an electrical fire?"

"I did," he said. "Just last night. I thought—I thought that's why you were here?"

"Why would I come over because of a fire?"

"I called your house. I left a message with your father. Or tried to. He was very rude." He paused. "I'm sure it's because of his injury."

My mind raced. The Emperor had called? What about? I asked him.

"Come see," he said.

I followed him into the music room. The smell of electrical burning, and damp wood, got stronger with every step. He opened the door, and I gasped.

Black scorch marks decorated the walls on one side of the room. Two of the black boxes on the recording table in the middle of the room had melted, almost.

"What happened?"

"I'm not sure, but I have my suspicions. I was away for the day. I called a tree man out to . . . finish the job your father started for me." I looked away, wondering if the tree guy had told him what he'd said to me. That Dad had messed up his orchard.

"You think he started the fire?"

"Not intentionally, no," Mr. King said. "A branch hit a line.

The power to the whole house was affected. There was a problem with the wiring.

"I can't believe it's gone," he said. "I only had it for a few days. And now I'll have to record it all over again." He kept touching the burned knobs and dials like he could rewind the fire that had melted them all.

"I'm sorry about the fire. But I came for a job. I need money," I said. "We're going to be evicted if I can't get five hundred dollars."

"What?" His head jerked up.

"Money," I said. "I need to earn some money."

At the word *money*, he smiled. "Money? Yes, of course, you can have another five hundred dollars. More, if you can get her to sing twice." His eyes lit up. "I would pay a thousand for two songs. I'll record it on my new computer. Bought one in the city yesterday. This time I'll store the recordings in some sort of external backup . . ." He went on, talking faster and faster, like a wind-up doll that had been given one crank too many, while I stared.

Get her to sing?

Wait. He was talking about Gayle. I took a step back, and he reached for me, his fingernails scraping my arm. He thought I was going to bring Gayle back to him to do—whatever he had done that had changed her? He thought there was any amount of money in the world that could make me even consider that?

I wanted to punch him in the face. I wanted to watch him bleed all over the floor. But I couldn't. I was here for a reason.

I was here for a job.

For a moment, I remembered the way Dad's eyes had flashed with hatred for this man every time he'd said his name. And how Dad had gone, anyway, every day, to work for him. So Mom and I would have food, and a house to live in.

The Jack Daniels? It was probably the only way he could stand the thought of going back every Monday.

I wished I had a drink of it myself, right then.

My stomach lurched, and I was afraid I was about to spew all over the Emperor's slippers. "Wait up," I said. "I'm not here about Gayle." I stopped myself before I said what I was thinking— *I would never, ever bring her back in this house*—and finished. "I'm here to work on your garden."

The Emperor's face changed again. "I have a gardener," he said slowly. "What I don't have—anymore—is a recording of your little friend's voice. And I must have that voice."

"Too bad," I said, hoping it didn't show in my voice that I thought he deserved to lose that recording—and worse.

"I said I'll pay you," he repeated. "I'll pay you a thousand dollars to get her to sing for me again."

"No, never," I said, backing up a few more steps before I spun on my heel and made my way to the front porch. I turned my head back once my feet hit the porch step, hoping he wasn't behind me, but he was. I repeated myself, louder. "Never again."

He followed me down, his eyes practically bugging out of his head. "You don't understand. Her voice—that voice is the only thing that makes me feel . . . happy." He paused. "At peace."

"No," I repeated, remembering Gayle with that half-melted stick of candy in her hand, that broken expression on her face. Remembering her head, bald in so many places. The pain in her eyes.

There was pain in the Emperor's eyes, too, but I ignored it. "No, sir," I said. "You hurt her. And there ain't enough money in every Emporium in the world to get me to bring her near you again."

"I've been near her, you idiot," he shouted. "The Cutlins brought her over this morning. But they couldn't get her to sing! I need her voice."

"You took that from her," I said, and my voice sounded like breaking glass. "With what you did. You just stay away from her. Haven't you done enough?"

"But—you have to!" the man cried out, grabbing at me as I backed down the porch stairs. "You don't understand! I—" His voice broke, like he was going to cry. "I promise—I want nothing else. If I can just hear her sing again, that innocence, that sweet, pure voice . . ."

His words were like a cloud of poison gas between us. I had

to get away from him before I breathed it in, forgot myself, and killed him with my bare hands. I ran, feeling his fingers peel off me. When I was halfway across the lawn, I turned to see him kneeling on the steps. I almost stopped. It looked like something was wrong with him. He was clutching at his shoulder, his left arm pressed up against his chest like it was paralyzed. "Get—back—here!" I heard him yell. His voice sounded weaker—maybe because I was far enough away. He had no power over me.

He looked broken, kneeling there. As broken as Gayle. As broken as my dad.

I slowed down when I got out to the road. The black dog that had been hanging around all summer was running in the ditch, steady and sure, back the same way I'd come. It didn't even turn its head to look at me, just loped faster with every step. Like it was late for an appointment, or something. Like it had a meeting with the Emperor.

I hoped it bit him, right on the face. I hoped it tore out whatever tiny scrap of coal the man had for a heart, and ate it in front of him.

I ran home, stopping on the porch. The smell of cooking bacon and cinnamon rolls drifted through the screen. My stomach growled.

For some reason, the house didn't feel like home anymore. Was it my home? Dad had told me not to come back until I had the money.

Had he meant it?

"Boy?" I heard a voice from inside. "Get in here." I waited, wondering why he was calling. To yell at me? Was he planning to punish me more? I didn't know if I could take it. I pressed my hand up to my heart, felt it *thump-da-dump* in agreement.

But then Dad said, "Come on now. Breakfast," and I knew. It was going to be all right, somehow.

Somehow.

Chapter 25

"We got a call," Mom said, while I was eating my second plate full of bacon and my fourth cinnamon roll. They were the ones Isabelle and Ernest's mom had made, I knew. I recognized the recipe—and her cinnamon-roll tray—from the church potlucks. They must have come by that morning, while I was out. I opened the fridge to look for something to drink and saw they'd filled it, too. Mom sure hadn't bought all those name-brand juices and milks. I swallowed a lump of cinnamon roll, washed it down with Tropicana Pure Premium, and asked, "Who called?"

Dad answered from the other room. "A customer," he said, and coughed. "They got a job for us."

Mom looked worried. She laid a hand on my arm. "It would be for you, mostly," she said. "Your dad isn't cleared to lift anything, or work just yet."

I got it, then. They weren't going to bring up the missing

money, as long as I did what needed to be done to make it right. My heart ached, swelling with gratitude. Somehow, I was getting another chance. "I . . . I'll try my best, Dad."

"I can tell you what to do," he called. "Teach you. You're strong enough to fill in for your old man for a couple of days, that's for sure. Plenty strong."

"What kind of a job?" I asked around a mouthful of bacon. The neighbors and church folks were obviously already taking care of us, with the food and rides to the hospital. Maybe Mom had let one of them know about our eviction notice. I bet some of the congregation members had come up with some "emergency brush clearing" that needed me and my dad. My guess is that the pay would be exactly five hundred dollars. Exactly what we needed to make rent.

I was right, almost. "It's taking down a tree," Dad said from the other room. "Just one. But they're paying five hundred and fifty dollars."

"That's a lot," I said. I felt a little shaky at the thought of cutting down a tree by myself. I set down my fork, carried my plate to the sink, and went in to see Dad. Mom was sitting right by him, unwrapping the bandages from his arm. I tried not to look at whatever was underneath all those layers of white, but I could see bloodstains showing up as she unrolled.

"Well, I told them we'd till up the soil for the garden, too, and work on some of the other trees they got. In the next few weeks."

I turned away, fiddling with my shoelace. "You think I can cut a tree by myself?" I'd only ever used the chain saw on small stuff, saplings and junk cedars. And sometimes, the saw had gotten stuck on a bigger cedar, and I'd had to call Dad to come to my rescue and work it loose. I peeked at his face; it looked like he was remembering those same times. But he didn't say anything. Didn't come to my rescue this time.

He just mumbled, "Yep."

I was scared, but I knew—this was what I had to do to keep a roof over our heads. To make sure Mom didn't have to wonder where we were going to live. To make Dad proud of me again. I swallowed. "When?"

"Tomorrow," Dad said. "I called the landlord. He'll give us that long to get the rent in."

"Where's the job?" I asked.

With the way things had been going, his answer shouldn't have surprised me. But stupid as I was, I had thought things couldn't get any worse than they were.

"The Cutlins'," Dad answered. "We're going to take out that sycamore so Verlie Cutlin can have her garden."

I didn't say anything for a while. I listened to Mom unwrapping his bandages, putting new ones on, coaxing him to take his pills. Mopping up when he dribbled water down his front. I didn't turn around; I didn't want them to see my face.

"Mom?" I said after a while, and stood. "I need to go out."

"Okay," she said. "Don't be late. I'm going to try to move your dad into the bedroom. I may need some help."

I looked down at the top of her head. The part was perfectly straight, as usual. But the hairs coming out from it weren't light brown, like I always remembered. They were salt-and-pepper gray and brown. Had that happened in the past week? Or had I just not noticed she had been getting older, sadder, every day for months now?

I wondered if my hair had started to go gray, too. I sure had felt enough misery to make it that way.

I wanted to sit on her lap, curl up like a little boy, and tell her why I couldn't cut down Gayle's sycamore. Tell her all the things I'd done, the thing the Emperor had done, to that girl. I wanted to take Mom by the hand and lead her up to the tree, have her listen to Gayle sing.

But I didn't say a word. I remembered a thought I'd had weeks before: *I would eat ground glass if it would make Mom better.*

I still would, I knew. But the thing was—eating glass wouldn't hurt anyone but me. Cutting down that tree?

That was going to kill Gayle.

I had to talk to her.

"I'll be back for supper," I said, and kissed the top of Mom's head, right where the gray hairs fountained out the most. "I promise."

Not that my promises counted for a lick, of course.

Chapter 26

When I got to the Cutlins', Jeb was out in the yard. He saw me coming and walked over to the side of the house to pick up a big stick. *Smart,* I thought. But I held up both hands. "I'm not here for trouble," I said. "I just need to get a look at the tree."

"The one your dad and you are going to take out?" he asked. "Funny how two weeks ago, your dad wouldn't touch the job for less than seven hundred. But now he'll do it for five and a half." He spat on the ground, reminding me of his mom. "Guess things have changed."

"Yeah," I said, my mind flickering across all the changes that had taken place over the past few weeks. "They have."

"Well, go on back," Jeb said, letting his stick fall against his side. He seemed almost disappointed I wasn't going to fight him. I didn't know how to tell him I didn't have any fight left. I felt like I'd already been beaten, over and over, with a stick the size of the whole world.

There were no birds in the backyard. Not a single grackle or crow, not even a hummingbird zipping past on its way to one of Mr. King's feeders.

Except for one small Nightingale. And from what I could see, her hair was all cut—or shaved?—off.

She was sitting in the top of the sycamore tree, her eyes on the sky. I wondered what she was looking at; there wasn't a cloud in sight. I made sure to step on some dry leaves, so she would hear me coming. I didn't want to startle her.

She didn't move, didn't even look down when I called up. "Hey, Gayle. You all right?"

A small huff of sound—was it a laugh?—broke the still, hot air. "No," she said.

"Come down?" I asked, not sure where to start. But I knew I didn't want her up there, in the boughs, when I told her the news. "Please?"

I watched as she slowly unfolded her legs and started the long climb down. Every step was tentative, like she didn't trust her tree anymore. Every handhold she took on a branch, she tested twice. She even stopped once and looked at the ground, like she was afraid.

I'd never seen her look afraid when she was in her tree.

Finally, she landed on the ground next to me, her knees

buckling. Mulch and bits of leaves came up in a small cloud around her feet, making her cough. I kneeled down next to her.

"I'm sorry about your nest," I said. "I wish I could have been here to protect it."

She didn't speak, just nodded. I looked down at the top of her head, at the bald scalp that looked so much like a baby bird's. I could almost see the veins through the stubble. I could see scratches, scraped places where either the razor or her own fingers had burned the skin.

"Oh, Gayle," I said, reaching out to pat her head, feel that soft hair—what was left of it—under my fingers. "What happened to you?"

"Tree!" She sobbed, and thrust herself against me, her arms wrapping around my legs, knocking me over into the dirty mulch with her. I tasted the bitterness of dead leaves on my tongue, swallowed the dust down until I coughed, too. She didn't say anything else, just let me hold her.

"Shhh," I whispered. "Shh."

Her whole body shook so hard, I was afraid she was having a seizure. How could I add anything more to her sadness?

But I had to tell her. Had to warn her, so it wouldn't take her by surprise. That would be worse.

"I have to tell you something," I said after a few seconds. "Something bad."

She still didn't speak. But she raised one thin shoulder and let it fall, like she was ready for me to get on with it.

"I don't expect you to understand," I said, trying to find the right words. "And I don't expect you'll ever forgive me. I won't blame you, Gayle. Not one bit." Her shaking stopped, like she was holding her breath, holding still for the final blow.

"I was supposed to give that money, that five hundred dollars, to the landlord. And I didn't. And now it's gone, to Mrs. Cutlin. And my dad's hurt, and my mom's—" I broke off, tears welling up in my throat. "Anyway," I went on when I could. "I have to make it up to them, so we can stay in our house. I have to do this job, Gayle. Dad already told them I would.

"I have to cut down your tree."

She let out a breath, sighing. There was—almost—music in the sound. Then, soft as a far-off breeze, two words: "I know."

Her arms tightened around my legs, and I felt hot tears splashing on my ankle from where she crouched. "I know, Little John."

I didn't ask her to forgive me. I knew better than that. But as I sat there holding her tight, running my hand on the top of her head, I wished I could think of something to do—some way to show her how I felt. How bad I felt for taking her to Mr. King. For giving Jeb a reason to destroy her nest. For cutting down her tree. For not being there when she fell, over and over.

But nothing came to mind.

. . .

That night, I sat next to Dad as he watched the news—or tried to. The TV kept cutting in and out, like it was about to die.

"I wish we didn't have to cut that sycamore down," I said during one of the static-filled pauses in the game. "That's the one Gayle sits in."

"Got no choice, boy," Dad said. "We need that money."

"I promised her," I said, softer. "I promised I wouldn't let you cut it down."

Dad let out a laugh. "Well, then that's fine. I ain't cutting it. You are."

"Isn't there something else we can do?" I asked, trying one last time. But I knew it was hopeless. Dad smacked me on the side of my head with his left arm.

"No more of that. You got us into this mess, you're going to get us out."

"This is all my fault," I said. It was strange. I'd thought the words so many times, I didn't think they would sound different, coming from his mouth. But they did. They sounded hollow. False.

"You got that right," he said, not looking away from the flickering screen.

"All of it?" I asked.

He didn't answer, just grunted. Close enough to a *yes*.

I stood up, angry now. "Really, Dad?" I said, trying not to show everything I was feeling on my face, like he did.

But he wouldn't even look at me. He was more interested in the television than his son.

My voice came out as hard as his had ever sounded, and just as deep. "Really? Funny thing is, I don't remember drinking away the rent money last week. I don't remember spending all the money Mr. King paid us on beer and bourbon." I stepped back as he made a fist.

"You shut up now, boy," he said. "You're the one that lost the rent money—"

I cut him off. "No, Dad. That wasn't rent money I 'lost.' That was hush money. Money Mr. King gave me so he could get Gayle alone. So he could get her alone, make her sing. Money you shouldn't have taken. Did you know she can't sing now? She told me he stole her voice. You should have thrown that money back in the old man's face. But you—you scraped it off the ground, like a dog."

Dad's face had turned purple. For a second, I thought he might have had a heart attack; he couldn't speak. But then his breath hissed out between his teeth. "That's a boy talking. It's time you learned a hard truth, son. Being a man ain't about doing what you like. It ain't about being particular where your rent money comes from. You see a chance, you take it, to support your family."

I said a word I'd never said in front of him, I was so sick of listening to his excuses. "I'm not going to do it," I said. "I'm not going to cut down that tree. It's all she's got left."

He took another breath, and started to rise off the sofa. His face twisted with the pain of moving too suddenly, though, and he fell back on the cushions. Mom called from the bedroom—"Boys? What's going on out there? John, are you all right?"

He scowled at me and bit out one final comment. "Maybe I did spend money we needed. Maybe you did, too. Now all we got is this chance to keep our home. You going to give that up, for what? A tree? A girl? Is she more important than your own mother?"

Mom walked into the room then, frowning at us both. Ribbons trailed from her fingers, and her eyes were glassy. "Have you boys seen Raelynn?" she asked. "I need to braid her hair."

"No," I said, answering both of them at once. Then, to Mom, "I'll go out and look for her." She kissed me, cool lips on my hot cheek, and said thank you.

I had to get out of there, had to get away. But I didn't have anywhere to go. I sat on the porch, listening to the cicadas hum, the far-off birds twitter themselves to sleep in nests that still clung to their tree homes. Every sound traveled in the still air.

I listened to Mom and Dad talk about me.

"You're awful hard on him, John," Mom said.

"Have to be," Dad grunted.

I wanted to laugh. Of course he would say that, think that. God forbid he ever be soft on me. I might turn into a girl. Or the kind of boy who made friends with little bird-girls.

"Why?" Mom asked the question I was thinking. I strained to hear Dad's answer when it came.

His voice was rough, and low. "It's all I got for him, Mary. Teaching him how to work hard? How to do the hard things? It's all I got to give." He laughed, a bitter, short sound. "I sure as hell ain't passing down a fortune to him when I die. Look at this place. I haven't even been able to provide a house for you." His voice broke, but he cleared his throat.

"That don't matter," Mom said. "We get along."

"Get along. That's all we do. No, Mary. I mean to teach him how to be a man. And hope he'll be a better one than me." There was a sound of cushions moving. "Now I got to get to sleep," Dad said. "Tomorrow's going to be a long day."

Chapter 27

The next morning, Gayle wasn't there when Mom drove me and Dad in the truck to the Cutlins'. Or if she was, I didn't see her. I hoped she wasn't home. I could hear the TV playing loud inside the house.

Maybe she wouldn't hear the saw at all.

Verlie Cutlin was standing by the door of the truck, arguing with Dad through the open window about paying a kid to do a man's work. "I'll guarantee his work," I heard Dad say. "He's as much a man as I am." I saw Jeb watching out the living room window. He made a face at me, then twitched the curtain shut.

Mom drove the truck right into the Cutlins' backyard. I could feel the tires squelching in the boggy ground. I hoped it wouldn't get stuck—I'd hate to try and shift the truck without Dad's help. But it made it through, all the way to the side of the wide lawn. Mom parked it a good ways from the sycamore. I got the chain saw out of the truck bed while Dad maneuvered out of the cab. He moved slowly, like he was a hundred years old.

"Now, you remember what we talked about at breakfast?" Dad asked me as I checked the pull on the saw. It was greasy and black. I made sure the chain guard slid back and forth without a hitch, and walked over to the base of the tree.

"Yes, sir," I said. "I'm to cut here." I nicked the place on the trunk with the blade, an easy height for me to saw. It would leave a sizable stump, but we could cut a second time and burn it out the next day. "At this angle, right?"

Dad nodded when he saw how I was pointing the saw. "Notch it there," he said, leaning close to the tree. He was panting from the pain of moving his arm.

"I got it, Dad," I said. "You go sit down."

I don't know why I'd hoped it would go fast, the cutting. I guess I kept hoping something would happen to stop it all. That it would start raining, maybe, or Dad would yell out, "No, stop! I've changed my mind. We can get the money some other way."

But none of that happened.

When the saw met with the tree, I jerked back. The wood felt so much thicker, stronger, than the trees I'd cut before. More real, somehow.

The chain saw screamed when I cut the first notch. When I cut the second time, I thought I heard something else, someone else, screaming, inside the house.

It's just the TV, I told myself.

"Good. Now make sure you step back when you cut through," Dad shouted out behind me.

I nodded, wiping my face on my sleeve, hoping Dad and Mom would think it was sweat I was clearing away.

I was scared on that last cut. If I did it poorly, the tree might fall the wrong way. Might fall toward the truck, or the fence, and then there wouldn't be any money for all the work.

No reason for me to have cut down Gayle's tree.

I swallowed, and set the chain into the wood again. The wood screamed underneath the saw. Before I could finish the cut, the trunk started to go, and I stepped back—careful, slow, making sure the chain saw was out of the way, like Dad had told me. The tree leaned over in the sky, then raced toward the ground with a whoosh of leaves and green, fuzzy seedpods falling like oversized raindrops around my head.

I stepped back one more time as the tree met the ground.

"Perfect," Dad said from behind me. His voice sounded tired. "Let's cut it into two-foot lengths, or smaller. The Cutlins want them stacked along the south side of the house to season for firewood." He coughed. "Maybe we can do that tomorrow."

"No," I said. I wasn't going to leave the tree laying across the yard like that, for Gayle to look out and see all night long. "You go on home. I got this."

I thought Dad was going to argue with me, but Mom took

him by his good arm and led him back to the truck door. "I'll be back in an hour," Mom said softly. "You be careful."

"I will," I promised. I watched Mom move across the lawn, over to Mrs. Cutlin, who handed her a stack of crumpled bills. I had a feeling, if I saw them close up, most of them would be marked from small branches, stained with chlorophyll from sycamore leaves. There might even be a candy wrapper in the stack.

I turned away, mopped at my face again, and got back to work.

No birds sang that afternoon. It was fitting.

Chapter 28

I slept the next day away. Mom came in to check on me at ten in the morning. She felt my head and told me not to get up. She thought I was sick, maybe because of the sunburn. I did feel sick, and my face was hot.

I was sick, sure. Sick at heart. My stomach felt like I'd eaten bricks, my chest like one had landed on it and was crushing the breath out of me.

My face burned. I got up to go to the bathroom, and stared at it in the mirror. It looked just like I felt inside. Raw, blistered, red as the devil.

I wondered: Was it possible to be so ashamed of yourself, your face would stay red for the rest of your life?

Ernest came over while I was in there. I heard Mom tell him I was too sick to come to the door, heard his footsteps as he went back to his house.

His birthday was over. I hadn't even called him on the phone. Maybe . . . maybe I could do it now. I swallowed, wondering if he would forgive me for all those months. Might as well try, I thought, reaching for the phone, dialing the first phone number I'd ever memorized, even before my own.

One ring, two. Then, "Hello?" He sounded older, his voice deeper.

"Hey, Ern, I heard you come over," I managed before I ran out of words.

Ernest hesitated. "Yeah, um. Hey, I'm sorry about your dad and all," he said after a few seconds.

"Thanks."

"How is he?"

"Fine, I guess." It was weird. We sounded like grown-ups talking at a coffee shop. Acquaintances. "I saw Isabelle at the store," I said. "She said you called to invite me to your birthday. Sorry I couldn't come."

"Yeah," Ernest said, his voice quieter. "She told me you didn't know. About me inviting you."

"I didn't." The silence between us hummed, but the conversation was still going on. Now Ernest knew—there was so much more wrong in my house than just Raelynn's death. There was my mother's craziness, my dad's accident. And me, the only one there who could hold down the crumbling fort.

"Hang in there," Ernest said after a few seconds. "You need

anything? Another one of my mom's Jell-O casseroles?"

I laughed, and so did he. She'd brought one over almost every day. It was like a reflex with her—someone got sick or hurt, she bought Jell-O and started mixing chopped fruit and vegetables into it. It was pretty gross.

"No, thanks. But tell her the celery–and–mandarin oranges one was good. Try and discourage the one with the ham in it, though, okay? Yuck." We laughed again.

"Your mom said you were sick. Why don't I bring you over my Nintendo? You could play the games I got for my birthday." So he knew. He knew I didn't have mine anymore. I wondered when he'd found out.

I understood exactly what he was up to. Making a peace offering. A truce. I needed something to offer him back. I'd been the one to blame for the months of silence. I looked around my room, wondering if there was anything I had.

What would Ernest want that I had? Nothing but for me to hang out with him.

"No, man," I said. "You hold on to it. I'll come over when I'm feeling better. You can show off your Nintendo ninja moves then."

He laughed, and suddenly, all those months of not speaking? They were gone, in a flash. The months of loneliness just became another part of our friendship, like one side of a diamond. Like treasure.

The line buzzed again, and I leaned out my window, staring at the darkening ground in the backyard. At the stump of the oak tree, and all the small branches that lay around it, scattered like pick-up sticks.

"All right," Ernest said, after a few more seconds. I could hear his mom's voice in the background, calling him. "Well, I gotta—"

"Wait." I stared at the sticks outside, my mind spinning. "There is something you can bring," I said. "If Isabelle has any. Can you ask her?"

"Sure," he said. "What do you need?"

"Pipe cleaners," I said. "As many as you got."

Ernest brought them over a few minutes later, and picked up one of his mom's Pyrex casserole dishes. He asked what I wanted the pipe cleaners for, but Mom was putting dinner on the table, and I didn't want to tell her. Or anyone, for that matter. They wouldn't understand.

No one would understand, except Gayle.

At least, I hoped she would.

"Did you hear?" Mom said at dinner. She passed the mashed potatoes to me. Dad's chair was empty. He'd worn himself out, Mom had told me, just going out to the Cutlins'. He had to sleep, so we talked low. "About Mr. King?"

"No," I said. "What did he do now?"

"He's sick. Dying, is what Trudy Lester said this afternoon.

He had some sort of an attack on the front porch of his house the day before yesterday. It was horrible."

I couldn't look at her. Had it happened when I had been there? Mr. King had looked sick. And I had hoped he would die. I'd thought I'd be happy if he did. But now, it just made me feel ill. I tried to swallow. "How?"

"Well," Mom went on, "he must have fallen—Trudy's son Paul is the paramedic, you know—he was all beat up and bruised. Paul said he thought it might have been a heart attack, but Mr. King wouldn't go to the big hospital in Abilene. He just checked himself out against doctor's orders, and went home. The poor man, he's all alone in the world."

I didn't say anything, just mumbled and finished my plateful of food.

So what if he was sick? If there was any man in town who deserved a heart attack, it was him.

I didn't care about him. I mean, I couldn't be blamed for a man having a heart attack, could I?

I excused myself from the table and went outside with my handful of pipe cleaners. I wasn't going to think about Mr. King anymore. I had a more important job to do.

And only one chance to get it right.

Chapter 29

The run to the Cutlins' house seemed longer the next morning. Maybe because the storm the night before had left puddles in the street I had to dodge, or maybe because I was holding a plastic grocery bag in front of me, trying to run slow enough not to knock it around and damage what was inside.

Maybe because I wasn't sure what Gayle would think when she saw me. Or if she would even come out of the house to see me at all.

Remembering the scream from the day before, the one I'd hoped was the television, I held the bag closer to my chest and ran a little faster. I had to see her, had to see if she was all right.

It was early enough that the streetlights were still on in town. By the time I reached the Cutlins' house, the sun had just started to brighten the edge of the sky.

I was about to knock on the front door, when I heard the

dawn chorus start up in the backyard. Mockingbirds, sparrows, chickadees—there had to be a hundred birds, and it was like they'd all picked that very moment to start singing. It gave me an idea.

I walked to the backyard, slowly, not wanting to startle the birds. Or Gayle, if she was there.

My eyes automatically went to the place where the sycamore tree had been. All that was there now was the stump I'd promised Verlie Cutlin I'd burn out in a few days, and above it, a jagged swatch of sky that shouldn't have been visible.

The birds were still calling like crazy, from farther back in the yard. I walked a few more steps, to see where they were perched. My feet squelched in the boggy lawn, and I felt the wetness rise up over the toes of my shoes, but I went on. There were a few trees near the back fence, a cedar elm and two red oaks. Not as big as the sycamore had been, but big enough for a kid to climb, if she was a good climber.

And those three trees were the ones all the birds in the kingdom were perched on, singing their hearts out. I saw a shadow move in one of them, too big to be a bird.

"Gayle?" I called out. "That you?"

The birds flew off. A few of them flew toward me, like they were dive-bombing a cat that was stalking their nest. One of the mockingbirds came back for three passes before I swatted at him and he lit off for the fence.

I stopped at the base of the red oak. "Gayle? I brought you something." I could see her shivering in the cool morning air. "Come on down," I said.

She didn't answer.

"Please," I tried again. "I have something to show you."

"Go home, Little John," she said after a few seconds. "You make me sad."

"I'm sorry," I answered. "I know I hurt you. I broke my promises."

"You killed my tree," she said after a few seconds of silence. "My friend. I didn't think you'd really do it."

"I had to."

A bird perched in the cedar elm mocked me with a whistle that sounded just like what I had said: *had-to, had-to, had-to.* Gayle made a shushing sound toward it, and it stopped.

"I know," she said. "I know all that. But it doesn't fix it." She sniffled.

She was right. Nothing I could do would fix anything.

"You won't come down?" I asked.

"I gotta look for my mom and dad," she said. "They told me if I ever got lost, to find my tree, and wait in my—my nest." She sniffled again, remembering what had happened to her nest, I supposed. "And they would come for me. They said they would never stop looking until they found me."

She was still talking about her parents like they weren't

dead. I didn't care, I decided. I played along with Mom through all her crazy talk about Raelynn. Everybody had to learn how to deal with death in their own way. If Gayle had to think she was some sort of bird, I didn't mind. I just didn't want her to be sad. "They'll see you up there, Gayle. Don't worry."

"No, they won't," she said. Her voice was so full of hopelessness, I couldn't stand it.

"Why not?"

"My tree's gone. And so is my nest."

"Maybe. Maybe not," I said. "Are you going to come down or not?"

"Not."

"Fine, then," I said, mostly to myself. I had known it would come to this, known the minute I saw her up in that tree, shivering and alone. "Time to man up."

I set my hand on the lowest crook in the tree, took the plastic grocery-bag handles between my teeth, and tried not to think about what I was doing.

A few pulls, a few unsteady steps, and I was standing in the crook of the oak, only a few feet below Gayle. I tried not to look down, knowing if I did, I would be sick, knowing I would remember what had happened to Raelynn—the fear that would freeze me. My mouth was dry as bone around the plastic handles, my palms slick and sweaty with fear. I took another step, and a piece of bark broke off the trunk and hurtled toward the ground. I closed my eyes and took a breath. When I opened them, I made myself look up, not down, and pulled myself to the branch where Gayle was sitting, the only branch up high that was sturdy enough to hold a kid.

I kept my weight off the branch as best I could, so it wouldn't break under her weight and mine. My heart pounded so hard it sounded like I'd eaten a woodpecker for breakfast. I was as scared as I'd ever been in my life.

"Little John?" Gayle's lips quirked up as she turned on the branch. I tried not to yell for her to be still, to be careful. The handles in my mouth helped keep the words in, though. I didn't want to drop the bag. "Little John," she said, scooching closer to me. "You're bald!"

I forced a smile around the handles, and muttered, "So are you."

She ran a hand over the top of my head, feeling the uneven stubble there. "We match," she said, and giggled. "Your head looks like an egg."

"Thanks."

"Where's your hair, Little John?"

Making sure my feet were firmly wedged into the crooks of the branch and trunk, I let go my death grip on one hand and took the bag out from between my teeth. "I made you something."

She took it carefully, like it might be a sack full of snakes or scorpions. "What is it?"

I smiled, wondering for the hundredth time if she would understand. "Treasure."

She frowned and tried to hand the bag back, but I gently pushed it over to her again. "Real treasure this time," I said. "Open it."

After a few more seconds, she did and pulled out what was inside.

I was amazed I didn't fall, what with her launching herself off the branch to hug me. But we stayed there, swaying for a few seconds, until I could breathe again. "Can we climb down now?" I asked. "Because I'm scared out of my mind up here."

Gayle laughed and shook her head. "We're only a little ways off the ground!" I looked down. "You're practically tall enough to reach, if you lower yourself down."

"Huh," I said. "You're right." I lowered myself by my arms from the crook of the branch and realized what she'd said was true. My feet were no more than ten inches off the ground. I let go, and landed softly.

"Well, that's embarrassing," I said and looked up. "I guess I forgot I was a giant now."

Gayle giggled, hugged my gift to her chest, and yelled one word. "Catch!"

Then she jumped, like a baby bird tumbling out of a nest.

And I caught her.

Chapter 30

Gayle opened the bag faster than a kid on Christmas morning. "It's the most beautiful thing I ever imagined," she said, sitting next to me. I ignored the damp ground under my shorts, the sounds of the birds all around us, overhead now—everything but Gayle and the nest she cradled. She pushed against me and held the small nest up. It was only about eight inches across, woven of pipe cleaners, twigs, and a few other things. But Gayle treasured it already.

"A treasure nest," I said. "Want me to tell you about it?"

"Yes."

I reached over her arm and pointed. "I made it out of sticks from a tree in my backyard," I began, then stopped. Should I tell her which tree? But she guessed.

"Your little sister's tree?"

"Yeah, that's the one. She loved that tree."

I cleared my throat. "Those are pipe cleaners from my next-door neighbor's little sister, Isabelle. She was Raelynn's best friend. They used to make pipe-cleaner animals, all sorts of stuff. They loved crafts."

"And the ribbons?" She stroked the colorful fabric that wove in and out of the pipe cleaners.

"Raelynn's hair ribbons. She had really long hair, and Mom used to braid it every day." We both stopped, and Gayle picked up the three stones that lay inside, instead of eggs.

"They're diamonds," she said, holding one up to the light.

"No," I said. "Those are smoky quartz. My dad gave those to me when I was five. I used to collect rocks. One day I decided I was too old for collecting things, and I threw them out. Dumb, right? My best friend Ernest found these three and gave them back to me last year."

Gayle stroked the inside of the now-empty nest. "And you made it soft," she said.

Her fingers ran over the silky lining of the nest. Then she reached up and touched my stubbled head.

"Well, I didn't want you to be the only bald kid in town," I said, settling the rocks back on the bed I had made for them out of my hair. Then I ran my own fingers over the stubble left on my head. I wondered what Mom would think when she saw it. She'd hate it. Dad, though? He'd probably think I was trying to look like a Marine or something.

It didn't matter what they thought. "It's just hair. Anyway, I needed it. Had to feather your nest, and I don't have real feathers. I don't think." I pretended to check my arms and legs, flapping my arms like I might take flight.

A giggle. "Thanks."

Gayle stood up slowly and walked toward the sycamore stump. When she reached it, she settled the nest on the top of the stump. The backyard quiet of insects and birdsong, of rustling leaves and dropping seedpods, filled the space between us.

"If I were bigger," she said, "I could fix everything. I could fix your mom and dad, and my tree, even. Maybe." She sighed. "But I'm too small. And everything's so broken."

When she said the word *broken*, every bird in the Cutlins' backyard flew up in a great swirl, like a curtain being lifted into the sky. I was watching their wings flashing in unison, so I didn't see what made Gayle cry out. But when I looked back, I saw him.

It was the Emperor. Or at least, it was his head.

He was on the other side of the fence, obviously up on a stepladder or chair. His face was red and sweaty, even in the cool morning. His hair hadn't been combed, and it stuck out in a half dozen directions, like the pinfeathers of a turkey vulture.

Gayle had scooted off the sycamore trunk and taken her nest into her arms like it was some sort of shield.

"I'm sorry to startle you," the Emperor said in a small voice.

"It's just—I heard you talking, and I thought maybe you would sing—" He broke off, coughing and gasping.

I started to tell him where he could go. "Get the he—" but Gayle stopped me.

"I won't sing for you," she said. "You're a bad man."

The Emperor coughed for a few more moments, his head disappearing. When I saw his face again, he looked terrible. Pale and red splotches spread across his face, like his blood wasn't flowing right. I remembered what Mom had said. He was dying.

I wanted to think *Good*. But looking at him, his face covered with tears, his eyes blood-shot and desperate, I couldn't muster up anything but pity and disgust. "You need to go home," I said, walking over to Gayle and pushing her gently behind my back so she wouldn't have to look at him. "You got no business here."

"Little John," he gasped, his eyes darting around like a bird in a cage, trying to find some way out. "I told you, I have to hear her sing. Just once, just once more. I'll pay you—I'll pay you two thousand dollars. Three!" he almost shouted as I shook my head slowly. His voice got hard. "Your family needs that money. You're going to have doctor bills I won't cover. And your dad can't work. What's going to happen to you then? All I'm asking is for you to bring her over one last time."

I could feel Gayle behind me, her hands woven into my T-shirt. "Three thousand dollars?" I asked, my voice dropping lower, then lower. "Three thousand dollars?"

"Yessss," he hissed, slipping again so his head dipped then came back up, a drowning man grasping at a passing branch. "Or more."

"Three thousand dollars," I repeated one last time. "You don't understand, Mr. King." I put my hands behind me, felt the soft stubble of Gayle's hair, calmed her shivering with a pat. "There's no amount of money in the world you could offer that would tempt me. Nothing in the world—not in every Emporium in the country—that would get me to ask her to be in the same room with you."

"But—" His eyes bulged, frog-like. "But—I'm dying," he said, his voice as full of defeat as any I'd ever heard. "I'm dying, you see. And I have to hear her—just once more."

"No," I said. I felt Gayle quivering behind me. "I'm sorry about that, but you can't ever be around Gayle. Never."

Gayle's arms wrapped around me, and she murmured a small "Thank you, Tree."

"You're welcome," I whispered back. I turned to take her to the Cutlins', when I heard the clatter and thump of someone falling.

The Emperor.

A thready voice, a wheeze of pain. And then—"Help!"

Gayle kept walking. I paused, wondering what I should do. He was alone. There was no one else around to hear his cries.

I had wanted him to die, planned on helping him get there

myself a few days before. But now, with him gasping for help on the other side of the fence, I couldn't do it. I couldn't walk away. Not even if he deserved it.

"Gayle, wait a sec," I said. "Stay here."

I ran to the fence and pushed myself up so I could see over.

The Emperor lay there, sprawling in his purple bathrobe, bare legs poking out like broken branches, arms clutching at his chest. There was blood on his chin—scratches from the fence or from falling. A chair lay to one side, its feet slicked with damp grass and earth. His eye found me. "Help!" he breathed.

I pushed myself up and vaulted over the fence. "Should I call 911?" I asked. He was having another heart attack, maybe. "Get the ambulance?"

His hand snaked out and wrapped around my wrist, hard. He couldn't answer, it looked like—his jaw was working, but no words came out. "Gayle," I shouted. "Go get Mrs. Cutlin to call 911."

"Okay," I heard, then the crunch of leaves and grass under small feet. I sat there, next to Mr. King, for what seemed like ten minutes. His hand was wrapped so tight around my wrist, I lost feeling in my fingers.

Then I felt a soft hand on my shoulder. Gayle had run round the fence, and stood there. She held her nest in the crook of one arm.

"You're hurt, Little John," she said. She traced one finger down the side of my arm, where I'd cut myself on the wooden fence as I'd vaulted over. It was bleeding pretty bad, but nothing I couldn't fix up with some butterfly bandages.

"It's no big deal," I said. "You need to get on back home." The Emperor was staring at her with those glittering eyes now. I wanted her gone, away from him. He might be dying, but who knew? A man like this was never safe.

"Okay," Gayle said. "I'll sing it better later."

Sing it better? I smiled. In those words, she'd gone back to being the Gayle she had been before I'd betrayed her. Before she'd been broken. If she thought she could sing me better— that she might sing again—maybe she could—

"For-forgive me?"

I jerked back, wondering how Mr. King had read my mind.

But he wasn't looking at me; he was staring hard at Gayle. "Pl-please," he wheezed, like each word was a torment to squeeze out. "Forgive?"

I twisted my arm out of his grasp and stepped up and away from him. Gayle held her arms to me, and I picked her up, careful not to crush her nest. She hid her face in my shoulder, and I shook my head at him for her. "Too late," I said. "She lost her voice, and her hair, and her nest, thanks to you." I took a breath. "And thanks to me. Just live with it."

I knew I would have to.

A voice inches below my chin said four words: "I love you, Tree."

For the first time, her calling me Tree didn't bother me at all. "I love you, too, Gayle," I whispered. "Let's get you back home. We'll find the perfect tree for your nest, okay?"

Somewhere in the distance, sirens wailed. Across the fence, Verlie Cutlin was shouting for Gayle, screaming for Jeb to find her shoes.

And in my arms, a little girl with the voice of a nightingale said one word: "No."

The Emperor's eyes closed, tears leaking from his lids. I took a step away, intent on taking Gayle back to the Cutlins. But she said the word again. "No."

To me.

"What?"

"It's just like Momma said. I got my nest, and my tree, already." She lifted her head. She wasn't crying. She was smiling, beaming. "It's all I needed. I can do it now. I can fix you, Tree."

"You don't need to fix anything," I started, but she put a finger up to my lips.

"I can sing again," she said, tapping her chest with her small fist. "My voice is back. I can feel it. I want to sing you better."

She opened her mouth, and magic filled the air all around us.

Chapter 31

It had to be magic. Even a kid like me, who had never seen a miracle or even a magician, could tell that.

Otherwise, how could I explain what happened next?

She opened her mouth, and a trilling series of notes spilled out, a waterfall of song. I closed my eyes, feeling her body grow hotter, like she was a miniature sun, heating up the air around us, warming my arms and chest, with rays of sound.

She grew lighter, as well, so light it felt like she was about to float out of my hands. *Was* she floating?

I opened my eyes, blinking through the tears I hadn't realized I was crying. "Gayle?" I whispered, but my voice was lost in a thrumming of wing beats, as hundreds upon hundreds of birds swirled and swooped through the sky above us, silent except for the sound of feathers and wind.

We all listened to Gayle's song, hypnotized. The notes told

a story, of a tree whose branches had cracked in a storm. Of a nest that had tumbled to the ground along with the limbs. Of a downy chick, broken on the ground among the dried leaves and gravel. The tree wept leaves until it was bare and empty, holding its last two branches up to the sky in a silent question . . . and then the song changed. A new bird, another chick, lost and swept along on a blast of wind, struggling to fly with feathers too soft to hold the currents of air, stuttered mid-flight, and began to fall.

Fell.

And landed in the crook of the tree's last two branches. Then, the bird and the tree sang together, a song of leaves and feathers, of friendship and protection, of soft winds and safety . . . and a nest of golden threads and silver twigs formed around them both.

For a second, Gayle snuggled deeper into my chest, like the bird in her song. I hugged her closer as the birds in the sky swooped lower and lower, landing on the ground, the fence, the bushes, even on our heads and arms.

Even on the Emperor, who was gasping, red-faced, but grew still as the birds settled silently on him, like a living quilt of feathers.

Gayle's voice began to echo then. Except there were two echoes, singing harmonies to her melody, deeper and fuller— and they came from somewhere near the edge of the Emperor's property.

"Gayle?" I burst out. It wasn't her voice at all for a second—her mouth was wide open, a baby bird hearing her mother's return—and then she strained against me and began to sing, louder, and clearer, and sweeter than ever before.

I heard the Emperor gasp as the birds all began to sing with her, as they began to fly in great whirling circles around us, a tornado of wing beats, heartbeats, and music.

I squinted into the wind, my eyes closing involuntarily against the close rush of feathers. The birds flew so near to my face, it felt as if I were becoming down-covered.

Down-covered—like Gayle felt in my grasp. I shifted my hands. It was true! She felt—softer. As soft as Raelynn's hair, softer even. My fingers brushed Gayle's neck. I could have sworn I felt feathers there.

Feathers along her arms and sides, fluffy down on her face. I wished I could open my eyes enough to see what was happening.

I pulled one hand away to cover my ears—the sound was so loud, it was deafening—and realized Gayle was being lifted out of my grip. *No, not lifted,* I realized, opening my eyes a crack.

Flying.

"Gayle!" I called, and strained to pull her back toward me ... but she was gone, taken up into the vortex of song and softness, changed somehow.

Or that's what I thought.

The birds landed on me, fell on me in a blanket of sound

and softness. I must have passed out. When I came to, I was lying next to the Emperor on the ground, Gayle's nest clutched to my chest.

And Gayle was gone.

Chapter 32

They all asked me, later, what had happened. I couldn't tell them. It wasn't the sort of thing a kid like me could explain, or that they would believe. Honestly? I had a hard time believing it myself.

It could all have been a dream. A hallucination.

But I knew, deep down, it was magic. And it was more than magic.

When Mom and Dad asked me, I tried to make something up they would understand. I told them Mr. King had thought he was having a heart attack, and I'd called the ambulance. "And then he got better, really suddenly," I said. "Like he'd never been sick at all."

Of course, that wasn't true. He'd been dying, almost gone, when she'd started to sing.

And then, when the birds had flown away, he had been

awake, and alive, and well. Healed, just like my arm. More than healed, maybe.

Changed, somehow. Maybe . . . forgiven?

He never spoke again, not that I or anyone in town heard. It was like the birds had taken his voice with them, up into the sky. And then, two weeks later, he died.

They'd found him in his recording room, with the windows wide open, a smile on his cold face and his eyes shut like he'd fallen asleep. Mrs. Lester's son, Paul the paramedic, had said he'd died naturally—but he thought it was still weird. The room had been full of feathers from all sorts of different kinds of birds, and thousands of sunflower-seed hulls and pieces of millet. Like he'd been feeding the birds inside for those two weeks, right in his house. When his lawyers read his will, everyone in town had gotten a surprise—the churches, the schools, and even my family.

No one could explain that. A few people, Mrs. Cutlin included, said he must have gone crazy.

"But why would he give us all that money?" Dad had asked. "You had to have done more than call the ambulance." I'd shrugged, knowing that anything I came up with would not be enough of an answer. In my dad's world, there was no such thing as magic. Unless you were talking about money.

I hadn't wanted to take the inheritance money at first. But then I thought, the Emperor was dead. And Gayle was safe from him, forever. If she'd stayed, I would have given it to her, if I could. But she'd . . . flown away. Or something.

The money worked its own kind of magic. Mom and Dad were happy. We could stay in our house now; we could buy the things we needed. We weren't rich, but we had enough for Dad to get physical therapy and for Mom to get counseling. Pastor Martin told me I'd done an admirable job of holding down the fort.

"But if you don't mind my asking, son," he'd said after church one Sunday, "you really have no idea why the Emperor would leave that money to you?"

"I guess he was just really thankful," I said, every time they asked how this miracle of money had happened. What had I done?—they all wondered—and why didn't I seem happy about it?

How could I explain to them that I would have said no to the money, if it meant I could keep Gayle? That I would give every cent of it back to have her again.

Everyone asked me about it—about that day. And not just about the Emperor. They asked about Gayle, too. The ambulance guys, the Cutlins, the police and the caseworker when they came. They spent hours that day, and for weeks afterward, looking for her.

"She ran off," I said. "She was singing . . . and then she just left. I couldn't follow her; I had to stay with Mr. King. I don't know where she went. I think she wanted to go home."

That was all true, and eventually the police stopped asking me about her. Her picture was everywhere for a while, on posters that said her name was Susan McGonigal. The picture must have been taken by the foster care agency at least a year before—someone had dressed her up in a ruffled shirt and brushed her hair. Gayle looked even younger and smaller in the picture, with sad, dark eyes and lips pulled tight. Someone put bigger, laminated posters outside the Emporium, and one at the post office, offering a reward and asking, HAVE YOU SEEN THIS GIRL? But no one had.

One good thing came of that, though. Mrs. Cutlin wasn't allowed to foster any more kids, since she'd lost one. That made me smile every time I thought of her.

Still, everyone knew there was more to the story. More I couldn't tell. And the strange looks kept coming for weeks, months. There were parts of the tale I couldn't even believe myself, and I'd been there when it all happened.

Eventually people stopped asking, and I didn't have to keep lying. It felt better. Not good, but better.

It was just . . . even with Ernest around, I was lonely. The same kind of deep-down lonely I'd been a year before, right after Raelynn had died. Only this time, not a soul understood what had happened, so nobody knew to feel bad for me. Nobody baked any casseroles or sent a card. Sure, everything looked all right on the outside.

The only broken part of my world was my heart.

Finally, a few months later, a bird outside my window woke me up. It was a birdcall I'd heard only once in my life, and it hadn't been a bird making it. It had been a little girl. I picked up the nest I'd made—the one I'd taken home and held on to, just in case—and went outside to the backyard, to sit on the stump of Raelynn's tree and listen.

But when I got there, Isabelle was already resting on it, listening to the same bird, that liquid river of sound in the night.

"Did you hear that, Little John? Did it wake you up, too?" Isabelle asked when she saw me walking toward her. Her clothes were dark, and the moonlight was so bright, it made her round face seem like a smaller, girl-sized full moon, floating in my backyard. Was she alone? I peeked through the chain-link fence and saw Ernest, yawning. His hair stuck out all over, and I smiled.

"Hey," he called. "You got this?"

"Yeah," I said. "You better get back to bed, get some rest. I'm going to teach you a serious lesson on how to drive Formula One tomorrow."

"You wish," he said, but stifled another yawn and shuffled back into his house, knowing I'd take care of his wandering sister.

Isabelle was staring into the sky, brows furrowed. Concentrating on the song. "What kind of bird do you think it is, Little John?"

"It's a nightingale," I said. I put the nest down on the ground.

"I've never heard one before. Have you?" she asked.

"Yes," I said, listening with her. "Once."

"Tell me," she said. "Where'd you hear it?"

"Well, it was once upon a time," I said. "In a kingdom not all that far away—"

"Little John!" Isabelle punched my arm. "Tell me the truth!"

"I'm trying to," I said, acting like her punch had really hurt. "Don't beat me up!" I leaned against the stump, and Isabelle leaned on me. "It all happened when I was just a little boy. A nightingale came to town. But no one recognized her, because she was dressed like a little girl."

"A girl like me?"

"Just like you. Except she had gotten lost from her mom and dad. They told her, 'If you can't find us, look for your special tree and build a nest. Then sing for all you're worth, and we'll find you.'"

"Did she find her tree?"

I laughed, once. "Yes."

"And build her nest?"

I ran a hand over the top of my head. "Someone built one for her. But it was good enough."

"Is it that nest?" Isabelle peeked at the nest on the ground that gleamed with silver and gold ribbons in the moonlight.

"Maybe," I teased.

"Did her parents ever find her?" Isabelle asked, and we stopped, as another nightingale, and another, joined in the song.

The night became almost unbearably beautiful as the three voices wove in and out and around each other, cocooning us in sound.

I wiped my face. "Yes," I said. "Yes, they did."

We sat there for a long time, until the singing stopped, and the only sound was the rush of wind through the wide leaves of the neighbors' trees—a sound I'd grown to love, somehow.

Like the sky itself was taking a breath, getting ready to sing a song to anyone who would listen.

Acknowledgments

In 2009, I wrote a picture book manuscript called "The Treasure Nest." Those four hundred words grew, changed form, and became *Nightingale's Nest* with the care and support of many people.

Thank you to the dear friends who helped me shape this nest in the early days: Shelli Cornelison, Rae Dollard, Bethany Hegedus, Cynthia Leitich Smith, Susanne Winnacker, and my agent, Suzie Townsend.

I owe a great debt to two insightful and skilled editors, Laura Arnold and Gillian Levinson. Thank you both for your perceptive comments and gentle guidance.

Throughout my life, I have been blessed with extraordinary teachers who built nests of knowledge, safety, and love for me, and later for my children. In gratitude and memory, I placed the names of many of them in these pages. If you see your name here, thank you forever for the gifts you gave in the classroom and beyond. I never forgot you, and I never will.

And always, love and thanks to my boys, Drew and Cameron, and Dave, who is my tree.

Turn the page
for a sneak peek of
another magical tale by
Nikki Loftin.

. . .

wish girl

Sometimes places are magical. And sometimes it's people.

Nikki Loftin

author of *Nightingale's Nest*

Chapter 1

The summer before I turned thirteen, I held so still it almost killed me.

I'd always been quiet. I'd even practiced it: holding my breath, holding even my thoughts still. It was the one thing I could do better than anyone else, but I guess it made me seem weird. I got tired of my family saying, "What's wrong with Peter?"

There was a lot wrong with me. But at that moment the most serious thing was the rattlesnake on my feet.

I'd just run away from home for the first time. *Possibly the last time, too*, I thought, staring down at the ground, blinking slowly, as if I could close my eyes and make the snake vanish.

I stood as still as I could on the edge of a limestone cliff, the toes of my tennis shoes hanging off the hillside, my heartbeat thudding hard and fast at the base of my throat, my neck stiff, and my eyes on my shoes. On the diamondback rattler, gleaming brown and black and silver-gray, curled around both my feet, looped across the tops of my laces.

Its head was unmistakably wedge-shaped, and its tail was light brown, decorated with eight rattles. I'd had time to count them; I'd been standing there for at least fifteen minutes, trying not to move a single muscle.

My mouth had gone bone dry. I swallowed hard, and the snake's head, which had rested on the top of my left sneaker near my bare ankle, bobbed up, black tongue tasting the air.

I held my breath.

For a moment, I thought of kicking the snake off my feet, running for it. Then I realized it was completely wrapped around my ankles. If I tried to kick it, it would bite me for sure. So far, it was just . . . smelling me, it seemed like. I remembered that from reading about snakes when I was little. They smelled with their tongues.

I hoped it liked what it smelled, because I remembered something else. Rattlesnakes could strike at twice the length of their bodies. So this one, if it wanted to, could bite somewhere close to my throat.

Boots. I should have worn boots. Or at least jeans, instead of my stupid gym shorts from sixth-grade PE.

Dark spots swam before my eyes. I had to breathe. I did so, slowly, trying as hard as I could not to make any sound at all, not to attract the snake's attention any more than I had.

The snake didn't strike, or move, just continued to lick the air. And then, a centimeter at a time, it laid down on my feet.

Like it was planning to take a nap.

I breathed slow and easy, or tried to, and wondered how long a snake's nap might take. How long was I going to be standing there, with a snake wrapped around my ankles, waiting to be bitten or to fall over?

Someone would come looking for me, I thought. I wasn't hiding or anything. They'd find me. If someone came over the hill and ran in the same direction I had for twenty minutes or so.

Out here in the totally uninhabited countryside.

I almost laughed. That was never going to happen. I was stuck out here, with nothing to do but wait, nothing to feel but fear.

As I stood there, trying as hard as I could not to rock back and forth for balance, I felt my shoulders begin to relax. There was nothing I could do, right?

Nothing but be still. Or die.

Chapter 2

I didn't die. I didn't even get in trouble when I got home four hours later. Turns out, it's not running away when no one notices you're gone.

"What did you do today, Peter?" Dad asked, passing me the mashed potatoes at dinner. "You didn't stay in your room again, did you, buddy? You know, some fresh air would do you good."

I didn't answer for a minute. What could I tell him? "Dad, I ran away and spent the afternoon trapped by a venomous snake"? Maybe he'd feel guilty. He'd been the reason I'd left, after all. Well, his drumming anyway.

Dad had lost his job and most of his hair in the past year, and he'd decided to relive his youth or something by playing the drums. He was "brushing up his chops" to audition for a band in Austin, he said.

That afternoon, he'd tried to get me to join in, handing me cowbells and triangles and nodding at me when I was supposed to bang on them. Father-and-son time.

I had told him the sounds gave me a headache.

I wasn't lying.

"You're so sensitive, Peter," Dad had said, disappointed in me, as usual. "You've got to toughen up."

I'd only heard that a thousand times. But for some reason, that day the truth had hit me. I'd never be tough enough for him.

I wondered if he'd believe I was tougher than a rattlesnake. I glanced up. Nope. He was wearing his perpetual "Why is my son such a weirdo?" expression. So I just answered, "I went walking."

"Oh?" Mom perked up and looked away from her lap, where she'd been typing something on her phone under the tablecloth. Probably trying to get on Facebook, even though it was practically impossible to get reception way out here. "Where did you go? Did you meet anyone?"

I thought of the snake and smiled a little. I didn't think that was what she meant.

My older sister, Laura, stopped spooning baby food into Carlie's mouth—or mostly onto her shirt and bib, as Carlie was sort of a moving target—and interrupted. "Are you kidding? Of course he didn't see anyone. Come on, Mom. You moved us out to the butt end of nowhere. There aren't any people for, like, fifty miles around."

"Laura, that negative attitude has to go," Mom argued. "I'll have you know, there are two boys Peter's age who live at a house only a mile away. This is a great place for us. It doesn't take any longer for me to commute in to the office, since there's almost no traffic—"

"Because no people," Laura interrupted, leaning back in her chair and angrily popping pieces of okra into her mouth. "No civilization," she growled through a mouth full of okra guts.

"No tattooed boyfriends," Dad added. "No potheads." He winked at me. I tried not to smile. I was the only one who'd heard, since Mom had started up again.

"Well, you're hardly one to talk about being civilized, Laura Elizabeth Stone." Mom raised her eyebrows. "Eating with your fingers? When you two go back to school this fall, I think you'll want to act a little nicer—"

That set Laura off again, on her favorite topic of having to attend a country high school where the biggest summer event was a rodeo, and 80 percent of the kids raised goats and steers for 4-H.

It was really different out here in the hill country, that was for sure. Different from our apartment in San Antonio, where we'd lived for almost eleven years. We'd only been in the new house for a week, but I could tell it wouldn't ever be home. There was nothing homey about it: a two-story, thirty-year-old wood-frame box with three different colors of vinyl siding and windows so loose they rattled in a stiff breeze.

I hated it. I think we all did. But we hadn't had much choice. Our old landlord had said that Dad's drums and guitars were driving away his other tenants. "Driving them crazy," he'd moaned the day he delivered the news that he wouldn't renew our lease.

I couldn't blame him. The noise of my family was unreal. The TV was on all the time, turned up loud enough to cover Carlie's constant tantrums and crying. My mom talked on the phone whenever she was home, or talked *at* the girls and me. When she didn't think we were listening to her—which was pretty much always—she just talked louder.

Like she was doing now, arguing with Laura. My head started to feel like something was squeezing it slowly, but hard. Carlie went from spitting food on her tray to crying. I picked at my meatloaf and thought of the valley I'd found that day. Where I'd met the snake.

It wasn't that far. Just across some fields of weeds, cacti, and a few scraggly trees and bushes that had more thorns than leaves. Then over the top of the hill behind that, past the fence made of railroad ties stacked diagonally on each other like enormous Lincoln Logs, and across the thin stretch of asphalt that was being retaken by grasses and wildflowers on both edges.

Just far enough away that I couldn't hear crying or yelling or drumming.

It had seemed like a dream. For the first time in years, I hadn't heard cars or trains, TVs or video games or people. Hadn't seen a roofline or even a plane in the sky.

I'd been alone for the first time in my whole life, almost. I liked it.

No, I loved it. Out there, my heartbeat was as loud as anything in the world.

Carlie shrieked. My head was the only thing pounding now. Well, that and Carlie's feet on the bottom of the table.

"Well, why couldn't we get a better house at least? One with high-speed Internet?" Laura asked. "It's like living on Mars."

"True," Dad agreed around a mouthful of salad. "That part's such a drag. Maybe we could get the cable company to hook us up—"

"We're on one paycheck," Mom hissed. "Mine. Did you forget?"

Dad lifted his chin in my direction, like I was supposed to say something.

I knew better.

But he didn't. He rolled his eyes—at Mom. "Like you would let me for one minute. Nag, nag, nag."

I held still. Laura did, too. Even Carlie paused in her tantrum. Then the world exploded into noise as Mom and Dad went at it, throwing blame and insults at each other as fast as they could, like they each were trying to win some invisible food fight.

And they didn't care who got hit.

"You chose this place without even consulting me, Maxine," Dad yelled. "Just because I'm out of a job doesn't mean I'm out of the family." His next word was a bullet. "Yet."

Carlie was crying full-out now, and Laura picked her up, humming some lullaby but never taking her eyes off Mom and Dad. She looked as scared as I felt.

Was this it? Were they splitting up?

My parents had always fought a little, usually in their room at night, after they thought us kids were asleep. But since Dad had been laid off eleven months ago—the same week Mom had gotten promoted to assistant manager at the bank—the yelling had gotten lots worse.

"You know we had to get away from the city, Joshua," Mom said, her voice low. "You know why." I felt her eyes on me, their eyes.

Maybe it *was* Dad's fault we'd been evicted. But it was my fault we'd had to move out here, away from the city they'd all loved. I knew that. Laura made sure to remind me every day.

Their stares burned into my skin.

"May I be excused?" My voice was a whisper. Too soft; no one heard.

The headache was getting worse, fast. It felt like something was splitting behind my right eye. Like my brain was under attack.

I held every bit as still as I had that afternoon, and I wished I was back at the rim of the valley.

And then, in my mind, I was.

My skin prickled. Like something was watching me. Something invisible and mysterious and vast. It seemed like the valley was waiting to see what I would do. I stayed motionless for longer than I ever had, wondering what was expected.

And then the valley took a breath.

Wind moved across the bowl, shifting trees and bushes like the land was a giant cat being petted. It moved fast, faster. It was almost here, almost to me.

Would the wind knock me over?

The hot air rushed around me, and the clatter of leaves sounded like excited whispers in my ears. Sounded almost like . . . hissing?

I smiled, remembering the rattler. I'd been so still, when it slid across my feet it had probably thought I was a tree or a rock. Thought I belonged there.

I stood for hours, snake around my ankles, fear in my throat. The breeze rose back up, pushing strands of my hair past my ears. It reminded me of when my grandma was alive, and she would stroke the hair back over my ear, feather-gentle.

The world around me came to life, like an orchestra tuning up. Some-

where to my right, a bird began to sing, a bunch of mixed-up trills. A mockingbird, I thought. Grasshoppers and frogs joined in. Something larger must have moved a little farther away, since I heard the sharp thud of rocks knocking together and sliding downhill.

The sun beat on my face, and I saw the shadows of clouds moving across the sky even with my eyes shut, as the light behind my eyelids went from red to black to red again.

Someone—something—was watching me. A shiver ran up my spine and made goose bumps prickle on my arms. It was the same feeling I used to get when my teacher would lean over my desk to tell me what a good job I'd done, in a quiet voice so no one else would hear.

Then something else sent a chill up my back. The snake was moving.

I opened my eyes and waited as it went from being wrapped around my ankles to slithering across the rocky soil toward a bush. And then, with a flick of its rattle, it slid under the bush like it had never been on my ankles at all.

I let out my breath and turned to go, my feet numb with the effort it had taken to stay in one place for so long. For a moment I wanted to shout, holler, and whoop as loud as I could. But before I did, a hawk flew by and yelled for me—screeched and wheeled right overhead, like it was saying hello. Or well done.

I waved with one hand, wondering why the hawk's answering call sounded like laughter. Why the sudden gust of wind felt like gentle hands pushing at my shoulders. Pretending to try to tip me over, the same way *my grandpa used to when we'd sit on his porch in Houston, just the two of us, him telling dirty jokes and me holding back laughter so Mom and Dad wouldn't come and hear and make him stop.*

Suddenly, the rattlesnake seemed like one of his jokes. Dangerous and funny and private. No one would believe me if I told them anyway.

"Helloooo?" The valley disappeared, and I blinked. Laura was waving her hand in front of my face. I didn't know how long she'd been doing it, how long I'd been staring at my plate.

It must have been a long time. Laura looked really worried, and her voice quivered when she asked, "What's wrong with you, Peter?"

For a
cozy-creepy read
that you'll
**GOBBLE UP
LIKE CANDY,**
check out

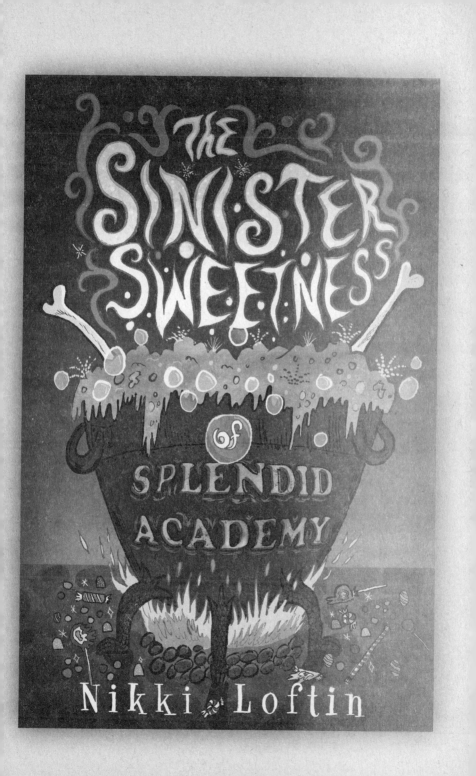

Nikki Loftin lives and writes just outside Austin, Texas, surrounded by dogs, chickens, and rambunctious boys. She is also the author of *The Sinister Sweetness of Splendid Academy*, which *Publishers Weekly* called "mesmerizing" and Kirkus called "irresistible." You can visit her online at www.nikkiloftin.com.